KU-211-474

Point

MYSTERIOUS CHRISTMAS TALES

Horror stories for the festive season

Includes stories by Gillian Cross,
Susan Price and Robert Swindells

■SCHOLASTIC

Scholastic Children's Books,
Commonwealth House, 1-19 New Oxford Street,
London, WC1A 1NU, UK
A division of Scholastic Ltd
London ~ New York ~ Toronto ~ Sydney ~ Auckland
Mexico City ~ New Delhi ~ Hong Kong

First published in the UK by Scholastic Ltd, 1992
This edition, 1999

This collection copyright © Scholastic Ltd, 1993
Inside illustrations copyright © David Wyatt, 1993
Cover illustration copyright © Mark Taylor, 1999

ISBN 0 439 01284 8

All rights reserved

Printed by Mackays of Chatham plc.

10 9 8 7 6 5 4 3 2

This book is sold subject to the condition that it shall not, by way of
trade or otherwise, be lent, resold, hired out, or otherwise circulated without
the publisher's prior consent in any form of binding or cover other than
that in which it is published and without a similar condition, including
this condition, being imposed upon the subsequent purchaser.

Contents

ACKNOWLEDGEMENTS

The following are the copyright
owners of the stories:

Home for Christmas © David Belbin, 1993
Squatters © Jill Bennett, 1993
The Crossing © Joe Boyle, 1993
Stockingfiller © Gillian Cross, 1993
Burning Memories © Adèle Geras, 1993
Hunter's Hall © Garry Kilworth, 1993
Christmas Game © Susan Price, 1993
The Dark Shaft © Malcolm Rose, 1993
Cloud Cover © Robert Swindells, 1993

CLOUD COVER

Robert Swindells

aura dawdled along the High Street looking at the festive displays in shop windows. It was two weeks before Christmas. Last year at this time she'd already begun to feel that special excitement the approach of Christmas brings, but not this year. The street was festooned with coloured lights again, and the shops sparkled at least as cheerfully as they ever had, but Laura's spirits felt no lift.

It was Mum, of course. Last year at this time Mum had still been her old self, endlessly rushing around, always in a hurry. Meetings, painting classes, coffee mornings and dinner parties. Constantly on the phone. Never a dull moment and not enough hours in the day. Up until three months ago, it seemed the only time Mum sat down for longer than five minutes was when she was working at one of her delicate water-colours.

Then early in September the illness struck. It was quite sudden. One day she was hurtling about as usual, and the next her strength had deserted her so that it was as much as she could manage to walk slowly from her bedroom to the bathroom and back. A virus, the doctor had said. Two weeks, three at the most and she'd be fine, but she wasn't. Not in September, nor October, nor November. In November Dad had taken Mum to see a specialist. At the hospital they'd done tests. All sorts of tests. They could find nothing wrong, but something *was* wrong. Something without a name.

Now Mum hardly ever came downstairs, and she never, ever went out. She spent a lot of the time sleeping, and when she was awake she'd sit propped on pillows with her eyes closed, listening to the radio. Now and then she'd try to read but reading made her nauseous, and of course she couldn't paint at all. She'd become a different person, and Laura found this both frightening and unutterably sad. It was why she was dawdling on her way from school where once she might have flown, and why the approach of Christmas had lost its power to thrill her.

The last shop on the row was The Gallery, where framed

6

prints of famous pictures shared the window with original works by local painters. Laura always stopped to look in this window. She paused now, gazing through the dusty pane at the dozen or so prints and paintings on display. No tinsel glittered in this window. There was no plastic holly, no artificial snow. The window looked much as it did all the year round, and in fact Laura had seen all of the pictures before, except one.

The new painting was a water-colour. As Laura's eyes came to rest on it she gasped. An ache started in her chest and spread into her throat and for a moment she felt she might cry.

It was sky mostly, but such a sky! Wide, wild and wind-wracked it was, cloud-clogged and bruised-looking. As she gazed, Laura could *feel* the wind which drove those clouds, shredding them, spreading them in rags across the bare, blasted moorland hinted at in the bottom third of the picture. She shivered, imagining herself for a moment standing alone in the midst of that howling moor, and she knew that if her mother saw this picture she would long to possess it.

For an instant, Laura's heart soared. She would buy the painting, carry it home wrapped in brown paper, hide it till Christmas morning and then . . . She saw Mum's face, heard her gasp as she herself had gasped. She'd be happy, wouldn't she? For a while anyway. They'd *both* be happy.

Then she saw the price tag and moaned softly to herself. Ninety pounds. Tears of disappointment pricked her eyes. She didn't have ninety pounds. Even Dad didn't have ninety pounds – not to spend on pictures, anyway. The painting was an original of course, hence the price, but still . . .

Oh, what's the use? It was as much as Laura could do to tear her eyes away but she turned and walked on. It's not fair, she thought. Mum's so ill, and that picture would've given her a bit of happiness on Christmas Day. Is that so much to ask? Is it?

There was a coffee shop on the corner of the next block. Laura had never been inside but now, on impulse, she pushed open the glass door. She knew why she was doing it and the knowledge made her feel guilty. The fact was, she didn't want to go home to a house tainted with her father's pessimism, the faint smell of sickness, the shadow of defeat. She bought a cup of coffee and carried it to a corner table. Except for herself and the girl behind the counter, the place was empty. Laura sat with her hands wrapped round the cup, thinking about the painting and about her mother. So distracted was she that she didn't realise she was crying, or that another person had entered the shop, till a shadow fell across her and a soft arm descended on her thin shoulders.

"Now, now, dear, whatever's the matter?"

"Huh?" Laura looked up, groping in her pocket for a

tissue. Her comforter was a smartish woman of middle age
with short, iron-grey hair. "Oh – I'm sorry. I didn't know I
was – I'm all right now."

"Are you sure?" The woman sat down. "Perhaps you'd
like more coffee?"

"Oh, no. Honestly, I'm fine. Feeling a bit sorry for myself,
that's all."

The woman gazed at her. "Sometimes it helps to talk, you
know – even to a stranger. Why don't you tell me all about
it, dear?"

She didn't want to. She didn't see how talking could help
at all, but the woman had a soothing voice and sympathetic
eyes and in five minutes Laura had told her everything.
When she'd finished, her listener looked into her eyes and
asked, "And how do you feel now?"

Laura smiled briefly. "A bit better." To her surprise, this
was true.

The woman nodded. "There you are, you see? No
trouble's so big it won't shrink with sharing." She smiled.
"Your mother *will* be well again, Laura."

Laura gazed at her. "How can you be so sure?"

"Trust me." She signalled to the waitress and ordered
coffee for two. She didn't speak again till it was on the table,
then she said, "I know it seems impossible at the moment,
Laura, but the clouds will blow away. They always do. All

we have to do is keep going till the sun shines again." She smiled. "Drink your coffee, dear."

Laura nodded and lifted her cup. How clever, she thought, to talk in terms of clouds and sunshine when she knows my mind is full of that fantastic picture!

It seemed neither of them had anything further to say, because they sipped in silence. When the woman excused herself a few minutes later and rose to leave, Laura said, "Thanks for listening. I really do feel better. I mean it."

The woman nodded, smiling. "I know you do. Goodbye, Laura, and remember – look for the sun."

"Where have you been?" Laura's father demanded as she walked into the house. "It's twenty past five." He was frying something, filling the kitchen with a pungent blue haze which made her feel sick.

"Nowhere. I was looking at the shops."

"Well, I wish you'd come straight home, Laura. There's plenty to do around here with me working all hours and your mother . . . the way she is."

"I know, Dad. I *do* come straight home, usually. It was just this once – the Christmas lights and all that. How *is* Mum?"

Her father sighed. "The same. Go sit with her, there's a love. I'll call you when dinner's ready."

Laura pulled a face. "I'm not hungry, Dad, thanks. I had something earlier."

Her father shrugged, busy with a fish-slice. "Suit yourself. They say eleven's a funny age. I expect you imagine you're getting fat or something."

Laura went upstairs. Her mother, propped on pillows, was finishing her meal. She smiled. "Hello, Laura. Good day at school?"

Laura smiled wryly. "Did *you* ever have a good day at school, Mum?"

Her mother chuckled. "I suppose not, dear – not at the time. It's when you look back it all seems to have been such fun."

"Well," said Laura, "all I can say, is, I'll be glad when *I'm* looking back at my schooldays."

Her mother smiled gently. "Then I hope you won't find yourself looking back from where I'm sitting, darling."

"Oh, Mum! I didn't mean . . ."

"No, I know you didn't, sweetheart. What I mean is, don't be wishing your time away. Enjoy what you have *now*, because we never know what the future has in store for us."

That night, curled in her bed, Laura thought about her mother's words. Enjoy what you have now. But that's just it,

Mum – I can't, because all the time at the back of my mind is *you*! Your illness, your rotten fate – and it spoils everything. Oh, I know it's happening to you not me, and I know it's selfish, but sometimes I can't help seeing it as *my* bad luck because it's messing up my life too!

Laura rolled over and cried quietly into her pillow. Just before she slept she saw the wild ragged sky in the picture and a voice in her head murmured, "Look for the sun."

Next day Laura felt tired at school. They were preparing for the festive celebrations, learning a new carol and rehearsing their play, but try as she might she couldn't enter into the spirit of things. She kept thinking about the picture, and the woman's words. "I *am* looking," she caught herself whispering more than once. "I'm looking for the sun." She didn't usually talk to herself. It occurred to her that she might be going mad, and at breaktime when Sandra Robinson asked her how her mother was, she burst into tears.

The afternoon dragged, but at last it was three-thirty and Laura set off home, taking a circuitous route to avoid Sandra Robinson. She was headed for The Gallery and she wanted to be alone when she got there. Why this was important – why she had to go there at all – Laura didn't know. All she knew was, she'd been thinking about the picture all day and praying it would still be in the window.

It was. There were shoppers all around but Laura didn't see them. She stood at the window, making a visor of her cupped hands to cut reflection, and there it was – the sky which had got into her head somehow and a wind you could *see*, raging over the moor. She felt again that ache, that lift towards tears. "Oh, Mum!" she murmured. "How I wish . . ." She broke off, staring more intently at the picture. She could have sworn she'd taken it all in yesterday, every detail, yet now she noticed something she hadn't seen then. There was a place in the cloudscape where light seemed to penetrate as a faint, suffused glow, as if some-where beyond those dark accumulations of vapour the sun might be shining. It was beautifully done – she remembered having seen skies just like that – and of course it must have been there yesterday, only she hadn't noticed. Oh, but how could I *not* have noticed? she wondered. It's the centre, surely – the whole *point* of the picture! How could I possibly have missed it?

She stood gazing, her breath making a fogged disc on the glass till the cold in her feet broke the spell. She looked at her watch and groaned. Twenty past four. More hassle from Dad if he's home. She moved quickly, threading her way through the tea-time crowd. Passing the coffee shop she glanced through its brightly lit window but the woman wasn't there and Laura felt vaguely disappointed.

When she got home, her father wasn't in yet. She went upstairs briefly to her mother, then hurried downstairs to cook. At least today there'd be no bluish haze. To her own surprise she caught herself smiling at this thought, and she hummed as she dumped pasta in boiling water and chopped a winter salad. Dad came in while she was doing this and smiled at her, which was something. Maybe, she mused, mixing oil and vinegar in a teacup, maybe I'm beginning to feel Christmassy after all. It's a little late this year but they do say better late than never.

Laura slept a little better that night, though her dreams were once more filled with stormy skies and a voice which spoke of the sun.

Mornings fell into a pattern. Seven o'clock: up, wash, dress. Look in on Mum, act cheerful. Down to the kitchen where Dad's had breakfast and is about to leave for work.

"Morning, Dad."

"Morning love. Don't forget Mum's breakfast, will you?"

"No, Dad."

"And do try to wash the dishes before you leave the house – the place was a pigsty when I got in yesterday."

"Yes, Dad."

"Oh – and remember to call at Tesco's on your way home, love. We're nearly out of bread."

"Okay, Dad."

"You'd better write it down now so you don't forget."

"Yes, Dad."

"And Laura?"

"What is it, Dad?"

"Give us a smile of a morning, eh? It's depressing enough around here without *you* standing there with a face as long as a fiddle."

"Sorry, Dad."

"Yes, well – you'd better get on or you'll be making yourself late for school again."

"Yes, Dad."

"'Bye then – see you tonight."

"'Bye!"

Eight-thirty. "I'm off now, Mum."

"Righto, darling. Got a tissue?"

"Yes, Mum."

"Lunch money?"

"Yes, Mum."

"Money for Tesco?"

"Yes, Mum."

15

"Left the place tidy for Dad, have you? You know how he fusses."

"Yes, Mum."

"Check everything's switched off before you go, won't you? And don't forget the bread."

"Okay, Mum."

"Have a nice day, dear."

"Sure, Mum – you too."

At twenty to four that afternoon Tesco seethed with glassy-eyed shoppers anaesthetised with piped carols and force-fed on Christmas, trundling laden trolleys between inflatable reindeer and chocolate Santas with a bare minimum of goodwill to all men. Laura grabbed bread, added a bunch of yellow chrysanths for her mother, and checked out.

Outside, she hurried along the darkening street. The plastic carrier kept banging against her leg and she hoped she wasn't wrecking the flowers. She reached The Gallery, dropped the bag between her feet and peered through the window.

There. It *is* there, the light. Definitely. I didn't just imagine it. In fact . . . She shielded her eyes as before and peered more closely. It's stronger, surely? I mean, if it was *this* noticeable I wouldn't have missed it the first time, would

I? It's stronger *and* more extensive. That whole passage left of centre is positively luminous, as though the sun might break through at any second. It was nothing like that before. It was dark. Those clouds were scowling at you as if to say, there'll be no sun today or any other day – the sun's dead. So how –?

Laura swallowed hard and shook her head. Water-colours don't change, yet this one has. Twice. Maybe it's changing all the time, slowly, like an hour-hand moving round. I'd like to stay here and watch but I can't, can I? I can't. She glanced at her watch. Five past four. All I can do is come again tomorrow.

There was something cooking but no car on the drive when she got home. Funny, thought Laura – Dad must've been home and gone out again. She opened the oven door. It was some sort of casserole and it smelled good. Bit ambitious for Dad. She unpacked her shopping, stuck the chrysanths in a vase, ran water into it and carried it upstairs. Her mother turned her head on the pillow and smiled as she entered the room. "Hello, darling!"

"Hi, Mum. I brought you these. Where's Dad?"

"They're gorgeous, darling. Thank you. Put them over here where I can see them. Your father's not back from work yet."

"But the oven's on, Mum. Something's cooking. Who —?"

Her mother laughed. "Me, Laura. I put it on. It's a chicken casserole."

"*You*, Mum?"

"Yes, me. I felt amazingly well for a time this afternoon – felt this sudden burst of energy – so I got up and cooked. Aren't you pleased?"

"Pleased?" Laura bent and hugged her mother. "I'm not just pleased, Mum – I'm megachuffed! I'd begun to think we'd never see you out of bed again." She straightened. "How d'you feel now?"

Her mother shrugged. "A little tired, dear – but also chuffed." She chuckled. "Not megachuffed, mind you – that'll be tomorrow – but there's definitely an element of chuff about me, and I'm cultivating it."

That evening was easily the best since September. Her brief spell in the kitchen had boosted Mum enormously, and when Dad learned of it he perked up too. For the first time in months, Laura went to bed happy.

As she settled down she remembered the words of the woman in the coffee shop and smiled. All we have to do is keep going till the sun shines again. Well, she'd been right, whoever she was. Laura had kept going – just – and this evening the sun had definitely shone. Trouble was, thinking

18

about the woman led on to thinking about the picture, and once she started thinking about that she couldn't get it out of her head.

They don't change. It's impossible. When I'm there – right there at that window – it's *obvious* the thing's different from last time, but thinking about it afterwards I know I must be mistaken. I know the woman talked about clouds and sunshine, but that had to be because I'd just described the picture to her. I don't remember describing it – I thought I told her about it without giving any details – but I must have. The only possible explanation otherwise is that she's psychic, and I don't believe in that stuff, and I don't believe in magic pictures either, so there has to be a rational explanation. But what?

Laura wrestled with the question till her eyes burned with tiredness and her sheets grew damp and wrinkled. It must have been midnight when it hit her. Of course! She sat up and gulped water from the glass on her bedside unit. Monet. Claude Monet. The haystacks. Now, why didn't I think of that before? Monet saw two haystacks in a field and he decided to make a painting of them, only he didn't do just *one* painting – he did four. Or was it five? Anyway, what he did was, he painted the haystacks the way they looked in the early morning, then did them again later when the light had changed and the shadows fell differently, and so on. The last painting showed the two haystacks at sunset. All of the paintings showed the same haystacks, but each painting was different in all sorts of ways because of the light. And that's what somebody's done with my cloudscape! They've made a series of paintings, showing what happens when a cloudy day turns into a sunny one. It's the artist's equivalent of the slow-motion sequence you get on the telly.

Yes, that's it! I haven't been seeing things and I'm not going barmy. Whoever owns The Gallery has this cloudscape series, and they're displaying them one by one. Tomorrow, just to make sure, I'm going to pop in and ask, but I know I'm right.

Laura lay down, smiled and fell asleep. Rational explanations are always comforting, even if they're not always correct.

The next day was a good one for Laura. She'd slept well, Mum had seemed quite chirpy over her breakfast tray and there was no more mystery attached to the picture. Sandra Robinson didn't ask how Mum was but Laura told her anyway. Better, thanks. Much, much better. Just to say the words made her feel good. The school looked pretty in tinsel, the carol was coming along fine and the hours flew. And when three-thirty rolled around it was great to set off

home and not wish you were going somewhere else instead.
She even felt like going *straight* home. After all, she didn't
have to stop at The Gallery. It wasn't as though she was
going to buy the flipping picture, was it? Fat chance. But on
the other hand, hadn't she stayed awake half the night
wrestling with the mystery? Hadn't she cracked it? Well,
then – she was entitled to the satisfaction of having the
correctness of her solution confirmed, and it'd only take a
few minutes, right? Right.

She arrived at twenty to four. There were plenty of
shoppers about. Laura hoped none of them would come in
The Gallery while she was inside. It was going to be hard
enough without someone barging in halfway through. She'd
looked in the window hundreds of times but had never been
in. There was a glass panel in the door, but a casual glance
wouldn't show you much. The interior always seemed dark,
and you wondered how customers could possibly examine
the pictures they meant to buy. The window was attractive
enough if you liked to look at paintings, but there was
nothing inviting about the shop itself.

Laura looked in the window and saw that yesterday's
cloudscape had been replaced by the next in the series.
Yesterday there'd been a bright, almost pulsating glow in
the vapour left of centre. It was so beautifully painted you
knew the sun was about to break through – you could feel it

out here on the December street – but it hadn't happened yet.

In today's picture, it had. The glow was still there, burning out of the haze, but now a single pale shaft of sunlight fell vertically from the cloud's dark belly on to a distant hillside. Laura saw how with one deft brushstroke the artist had bestowed luminosity on that hillside. It was a green-gold smear a centimetre long, yet it drew both the eye and the memory. You'd seen hillsides with the sun on them and they looked so *exactly* like that it made you want to weep.

No. Laura tore her moist eyes away. No blubbing. You don't have ninety pounds and that's that. It's time. Up the step, through the door, ask your question, home to Mum. Easy.

It wasn't easy, though. She hesitated on the step, trying to see through the dark panel, half hoping a customer would show up and give her an excuse to abandon her plan. From out here it looked like the sort of shop you sometimes see in horror movies – the sort where when you go in, a rusty bell pings and an ugly old guy comes shuffling through a dusty curtain and you just *know* he's going to turn out to be a zombie or a vampire or an alien or something, and when you try to leave the shop the door's locked and he's coming towards you, grinning a snaggle-tooth grin.

Don't be so stupid! It's a perfectly ordinary little shop on a busy street in a boring English town where nothing ever happens. It's probably run by a money-grubbing little wally with two chins and a ginger moustache who drives a Volvo and collects concrete gnomes.

So how come I've never seen anyone go inside?

Laura dismissed the question, took a deep breath, grabbed the door handle and pushed. There was no bell, rusty or otherwise, and nobody came through the curtain. The proprietor was already behind the counter, beaming. It was the woman who'd bought her coffee.

"Oh – hello – I —"

"Laura." The woman smiled. "You've come for your picture at last."

"No – no." Laura shook her head. "I told you. I don't have ninety pounds. I came in to ask something, only I didn't know this was your shop."

The woman arched her brows. "Does it make a difference?"

"I – guess not."

"Then ask."

"Well, it's just – there's more than one picture, isn't there? I mean, there *has* to be because water-colours don't change, only I thought – for a day or two I thought it *was* changing. Either that or I was going mad."

The woman looked at her. "I'm sorry, Laura – I'm afraid I

23

haven't the faintest idea what you're talking about. I have hundreds of pictures here but there's only the one cloudscape."

"Are – are you sure?"

"Am I sure?" The woman chuckled. "I ought to be, dear – I painted it."

"You?" gasped Laura.

"Why not me?" The woman seemed amused. "Don't I look like a painter?"

"Oh, no. I mean, yes. It's not that. I mean – look, I was so sure I'd cracked the mystery, and now —"

"Mystery?" The woman shook her head. "There's no mystery, Laura. I painted a cloudscape. A *single* cloudscape. It's been in my window all week. If you've seen changes, it's the way you've looked at the picture that's changed." She smiled. "Shall I wrap it for you? How *is* your mother, by the way?"

Laura shook her head. "No. I haven't got the money, you see. Mum's better, thanks. Much better."

"Good. I'm glad. And since it's my painting – my own work, I mean – the money doesn't matter, does it?" She began pulling brown paper from a roll bolted to the counter.

"Oh, please!" protested Laura. "I can't do that. I can't take your picture and not pay. It wouldn't be right."

The woman shook her head. "Then don't take it, dear –

24

let me give it to you." She fetched the painting, placed it on the paper and began wrapping it. "I don't have giftwrap, I'm afraid."

"It doesn't – I still don't feel right about this."

"Don't let it worry you, Laura. It's my pleasure, believe me. Here." She held out the neat rectangular package. Laura took it.

"Thank you. I – I'll never forget this, honestly I won't. I don't even know your name."

The woman shook her head. "I know you don't and you're absolutely right – you'll never forget. Goodbye, Laura. Oh, and don't worry about your mother, dear – illness is a thing of the past for her now."

Laura walked homeward in a warm haze of wellbeing. Not only could she *feel* Christmas – it seemed to her that she was included as never before at the very heart and meaning of the festival. She'd stopped believing in angels at around the same time as she'd realised there was no Santa Claus, but now her certainty regarding these matters faltered. It seemed to her she'd discovered one or the other, or maybe a combination of the two, running a poky little picture shop in the High Street. It wasn't till she turned the corner into her own road that she discovered how mistaken she was.

There were two fire engines, one ambulance, a haze of bluish smoke and a knot of people by the gate. Not our gate, said Laura's brain. Next door, surely? Nevertheless her pace quickened, and by the time her father intercepted her she knew and was running, half-blind with terror and with tears, towards her gutted home.

"Laura!" He circled her with his arms, forced her to halt, crushed her face against his shirt and tie. "Wait, darling. You mustn't go near. There's nothing to be done."

She cried out, writhing to break his hold. "Mum? Is it Mum?"

She felt his affirmative nod. "She was – she must have tried to cook, Laura," he said. "Collapsed in the kitchen. Mrs Atkinson saw smoke, but by then —"

"Is she —"

Again the affirmative nod.

"It's my fault, Dad. All my fault. If I'd come straight home instead of going to —" She broke off as the woman's last words came back to her. *Don't worry about your mother, dear – illness is a thing of the past for her now.*

"The picture – let me look at the picture!"

Her father struggled to restrain her but now she was wild. Desperate. When wriggling failed to free her she sank her teeth in his wrist, broke away and backed off, tearing at the wrapping. He made a grab for her but she sidestepped. The paper fell away to reveal what she'd known it concealed – a sombre, brooding cloudscape beyond which, somewhere, the sun lay dead.

She knew what she must do. She turned, clutching the picture, and began running back the way she'd come. She must find the woman – make her paint the sun! One stroke – one deft stroke was all it would take, then Mum would be all right again and Christmas could begin.

She couldn't know that already The Gallery stood empty, its window bare except for a square of card on which were scrawled the words FOR SALE.

STOCKING FILLER

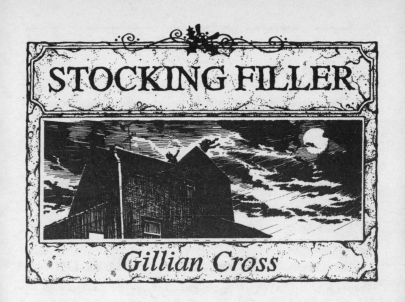

Gillian Cross

mogen knew Henry was going to be mean. It was the first Christmas since he'd married their mother, and any *normal* man would have wanted to make things extra-special for her and Paul. He should have been offering them trips to exciting places, and new clothes, and thousands of presents.

But there was no sign of anything like that. He hadn't even left catalogues around the house, or asked them for Christmas lists, the way their own father did.

Imogen tried hinting, but Henry just grinned.

"We like surprises best – don't we, Becky? And you and Paul will like them too, Imo. When you get used to them."

29

Becky chuckled, like a little idiot and snuggled into her father's jumper. Imogen felt like screaming. What was the use of a surprise, if it wasn't what you wanted?

But she managed to keep her temper – just about. Until Henry brought the Christmas tree home.

He carried it in over his shoulder, and Becky squealed with delight.

"Can I help you with the decorations, Daddy? *Please!* You promised!"

Henry grinned and dumped the tree into a bucket. "Don't see why not. Maybe Imogen and Paul would like to join in too. How about it, Imo?"

Imogen tossed her head. "I always do the Christmas tree. Every year. My dad says I've got better taste than most adults he knows."

"Imogen and I can do it together!" Becky said, bouncing up and down. "I'll go and get the things."

She raced off to the cupboard under the stairs and came back with a large, battered cardboard box.

"There!" She dumped it triumphantly on the carpet.

Imogen looked down at the box. "What's *that*?"

"The Christmas decorations. Look!" Becky flung the lid back, and began to scoop them out. "Here's the star that Mummy made. And my angel from nursery. And the tinsel from when I was a fairy in the play last year."

Imogen shuddered. "You're going to put *old* decorations on the tree?"

"We – I –" Becky looked up, and her smile faltered. "We always have these."

Henry put a hand on her shoulder. "I expect Imogen and Paul have got their own decorations, Spicky. It would be nice to have a mixture, wouldn't it?"

He gave Imogen a hopeful smile, but she snorted scornfully.

"We haven't got any old decorations. We always buy new ones every year. And Dad always lets – let me choose. This year, I want it all pink and silver."

"But –" Henry was speechless. And Becky looked horrified.

"Pink glass baubles," Imogen said briskly. "And loads of silver tinsel. I've seen a set of little pink lights like candles in silver holders – two sets would be just right for that tree. And Morris's have got some wonderful pink cherubs with silver wings. We could have twenty of those, and I'll make a pink and silver angel to go on top of the tree."

Becky's bottom lip wobbled. "B-but what about Mummy's star? We always have *that* on top of the tree."

Imogen shrugged coldly. "It's the wrong colour, isn't it? Look at all those red and green bits."

Big tears began to glisten in Becky's eyes, and she screwed

her hands into fists. Henry put one arm round her and one arm round Imogen.

"Listen, Imo."

"Imo*gen*," said Imogen sharply.

"Imogen. I can see you're good at choosing tree decorations, but we can't afford to buy new ones every year. Twenty cherubs and two sets of lights would cost – well, I can't begin to guess. Suppose I buy you just *one* cherub. If you're really set on them."

"*One* cherub's no use at all!" Furiously, Imogen wriggled out of his arm and stamped off into the kitchen.

Her mother was standing in front of the Christmas cake holding an icing bag, and Paul was facing her across the table, with his face bright red. Imogen marched straight in and banged her hand down on the cake board.

"Henry says we can't have a proper Christmas tree this year! We've got to use some measly old decorations out of a cardboard box!"

"Huh! That's nothing!" Paul said fiercely, before their mother could answer. "Mum says we can't afford an opera for our Christmas treat. We've got to go to a pantomime."

"A pantomime?" Imogen sat down suddenly. "But – we *can't*. Dad always took us to the opera."

Their mother let go of her icing bag and sat down opposite Imogen. "Look, you know how things are. I explained it all before Henry and I got married. There isn't endless money any more. We just have to have different kinds of fun."

Imogen scowled. "Like having Becky's mum's tatty star on top of the Christmas tree?"

Their mother looked severe. "Emily made that star just before she died. Becky needs to have it on top of the tree."

"Yuck!" Paul pulled a face. "Who wants to think about dead people at Christmas? They're not here."

"Your father's not here either," their mother said quietly. "Don't you –" she hesitated. "Don't you think about *him*?"

"What for?" Imogen kicked at the table leg. "He didn't even bother to come home from Abu Dhabi last Christmas. And he's taking Cordelia to Paris, so we won't see him this year either."

"I bet *they* go to the opera," Paul said gloomily. "I'm going to phone up and ask him to send some tickets. I'll say Henry's too poor to do Christmas properly."

"No you won't!" Their mother turned pink. "Henry can't help it if he –"

Her voice faltered and she looked up. Imogen swivelled round and saw Becky standing in the doorway. She looked as if she were going to explode.

"I don't care if my daddy doesn't earn much money!" she said fiercely. "At least he didn't go off and leave me, like *your* daddy did."

She rushed out of the room. For a second, Paul and Imogen thought their mother was going to rush after her, but she didn't. Instead, she glared at them.

"Look what you've done now! You're not to spoil Becky's Christmas. She's only seven, and it all means a lot to her. Be nice."

"What about *our* Christmas –" Paul began.

But Imogen had had an idea. She nudged him.

"Don't worry, Mummy," she purred. "We'll be very, very nice. Come on, Paul."

She pulled him out of the room before he could protest any more. By the time they reached the bottom of the stairs, he was spluttering.

"Why did you give in like that? I hate Mum going on about Marvellous Little Becky and telling us how horrible we are."

Imogen sighed, impatiently. "You won't change that by *being* horrible. What we need to do is make her take another look at Becky."

"How d'you mean?"

"Well, suppose *Becky* started asking for things."

Paul frowned. "But she never does."

"Yes, but suppose she did."

Imogen leaned forward and began to whisper in his ear . . . Half an hour later, she was up in the bedroom she shared with Becky, flicking through the clothes in the wardrobe.

34

"What are you going to wear on Christmas Day, Spicks?"

Becky brightened. She liked Imogen to call her Spicks.

"My velvet party dress, of course."

"*That* old thing?" Imogen raised her eyebrows, pretending to be surprised.

"It's my best!" Becky said uncertainly.

"But doesn't your dad buy you something new for Christmas Day? You poor thing! Why don't you ask him for a new dress?"

Becky looked miserable, not sure whether she was being teased. Before she could find out, Paul came in, swinging a silver chain.

"Hi, Becks. What d'you think you're going to get in the pudding this year?"

"In the pudding?" Becky stared. "What could there be in the pudding?"

"Silver charms, of course." Paul swung his chain right under her nose. "We've always had one, every year since we were born. I put all nine of mine on this chain. They're much too valuable to lose."

He dropped the chain into Becky's lap, and she fingered the little silver cars and dogs and houses.

"You got those in the Christmas pudding?"

"Aren't they nice?" Imogen pulled her charm bracelet out of the dressing table drawer and spread it beside Paul's

35

chain. "Look, I've got twelve. Which do you like best? The little cat's my favourite. Or maybe the silver buttercup."

"Oh!" Becky draped the bracelet round her wrist and stroked the cat longingly. "They're *lovely*!"

Behind her back, Imogen gave Paul a sly grin. Then she leaned closer to Becky. "What d'you think we'll get this year?"

For a second longer, Becky stroked the cat. Then she picked up the chain and the bracelet and held them out. "I don't think we'll have charms," she said sadly. "They must be ever so expensive."

"You could ask your dad," Paul whispered.

They could see she was tempted, but she shook her head and dropped the charms back into their hands. "He wouldn't like it."

Paul scowled, but Imogen didn't give up so easily.

"Well, why don't you ask *Father Christmas*, then? He might bring you a new dress, as well."

"Father Christmas?" Becky looked puzzled. "He only brings little things."

"Not necessarily," murmured Imogen. "It depends what you put in your letter."

"Letter?"

"Don't you write him a letter, asking for what you want?"

Becky shook her head, gazing at them with big, round eyes.

Paul sat down on the bed beside her. "Last Christmas I asked him for a new camera and a pair of Nike trainers and a laptop computer, and I got them all. *And* lots of other things besides."

"In your stocking?" Becky sounded puzzled. "How did they fit in?"

"Oh, we don't bother with stockings," Imogen said, airily.

"You don't hang them up round the fire?"

"No, we just put a box at the end of our bed. I had a new personal stereo and a leather jacket and six CDs."

"But –" Becky sounded even more puzzled. "Weren't they your big presents? From your mum and dad?"

"*Those* were round the tree," said Paul. "*These* were from Father Christmas. You know, the old man with the white beard."

Becky was still staring. Imogen sat down on her other side and put an arm round her. "You really ought to write a letter," she said softly. "We know it's hard for your dad this Christmas, having to pay for all of us. But *Father Christmas* won't be hard up. He could bring you really nice things."

"Why don't we help you write it?" Paul said. "We can make sure you get the spellings right."

They shepherded Becky across to the desk and knelt one

on each side of her as she sat in the chair. Paul took a pencil out of the tin on the desk, and Imogen produced a sheet of her own pink writing paper.

"Now," she said. "What do you want to ask for?"

It was harder than they thought. Becky wasn't used to asking for presents, and all she produced on her own was a list of three things.

a doll

some pink writing paper

a silver cat charm

"You've got to ask for more than *that*," Paul said. "How about a personal stereo? I'll spell it for you. P-e-r-s-"

"And a new dress," broke in Imogen. "What about a black one with a silver skirt?"

"And you could have a camera . . ."

They prompted and suggested and persuaded, until her list had stretched to the end of the paper. Then they stood up.

"Let's take it down to Mum," Imogen said. "She's good at posting them up the chimney." She gave Paul another sly, secret grin. It was all the two of them could do not to giggle.

When they went downstairs, their mother and Henry were in the sitting room, decorating the tree. Imogen pushed Becky into the room on her own and she and Paul waited outside the door, to see what would happen.

Their mother took the list and read it, very slowly. Then she put a hand over her face and sat down, suddenly, on the sofa.

"I can't bear it, Henry. Imogen and Paul always got spoilt by their father. Now they're making Becky as bad as they are."

Huh! mouthed Paul. Imogen went pink and leaned closer to the door, to hear what Henry would say.

He read the list solemnly, and then he looked at Becky. "You don't really want all this stuff, do you?"

"Yes I do," Becky said, importantly. "It's my Father Christmas List. *He's* not short of money, even if we are."

Henry thought for a moment. Then he folded the list up, very small. "You've got a lot to learn about Father Christmas, Spicks. Maybe it would be better if you didn't have a stocking this year."

"No s-stocking?" said Becky. She looked as if she were going to cry.

Henry crouched down and put an arm round her. "It's the best way, you know. Whatever you get, you'll be disappointed now. So we won't have them at all this year. We'll have a simple, plain Christmas. And next year we'll start out fresh." He raised his voice. "All right, you two?"

Suddenly Imogen felt very silly, huddled behind the door. She stepped into the room and tossed her head. "I don't care about a silly old stocking. Father Christmas wouldn't have brought anything good anyway. Not *this* year."

"Just a few packets of sweets," Paul said scornfully. "And a plastic toy to float in the bath."

They weren't going to show how much they cared. But they hoped Becky would. They wanted her to whine and complain like a baby, until everyone was sick of her.

But she didn't. She just bit her lip and went upstairs to play with her doll's house. And she wouldn't ask for anything else, however Imogen and Paul tried to persuade her.

She didn't mention stockings again until it was actually Christmas Eve, and she was getting ready for bed. Then she took a red-and-white striped football sock out of her bottom drawer and looked at it for a moment.

"What's up?" said Imogen. She was struggling to wrap all the presents she'd bought that afternoon. "You don't think Henry's going to change his mind, do you?"

Becky shook her head. "I just wondered . . . I know I can't hang this up by the fire, like I usually do. But – if I hung it up at the bottom of my bed, do you think Father Christmas might come anyway?"

"Not a chance," said Imogen spitefully. "No one's told him to call. If you want to catch him, you'll have to get up on the roof and wave."

Scooping up her parcels, she went off to put them under the tree. And on the way she went into Paul's room, to tell him what Becky had said.

"She really *believes* all that stuff about Father Christmas!"

"You should have encouraged her," Paul said. "Told her to hang up the stocking. Just imagine how she'd have looked tomorrow, when it was empty!"

"Splat!" Imogen grinned. She was sorry she hadn't thought of that. "Maybe she'll hang it up anyway."

But when she went to bed herself, the striped sock was nowhere to be seen. *Pity*, she thought. Climbing into bed, she drifted off to sleep, wondering whether she would get a present from her father.

She was woken up by a cold draught blowing straight on to her face. For a few seconds she tried to ignore it, burrowing deeper under the covers, but the cold air wriggled its way in with her, and at last she gave in and sat up.

The room was freezing.

Was the window open? She slid out from under the covers and padded past the end of Becky's bed to look.

No, it was closed. But as she pulled the curtains apart she realised that Becky wasn't there. The light from the street lamp outside fell on to tumbled white sheets. Imogen reached out to feel them, and they were icy cold.

Not again!

When they first moved in with Henry, Becky had been a terrible sleepwalker. Almost every night, she was found downstairs in her pyjamas, wandering around fast asleep. But she'd been much better for the last month or so, and everyone thought she was cured.

"Well, I'm not hunting for her!" Imogen muttered under her breath. "Let her freeze downstairs if she wants to!"

She turned to go back to bed, but another cold blast of air hit her in the face. And this time it came, unmistakably, from the ceiling. She looked up irritably and saw a dark square gaping over her head just above the big old bookshelves.

Someone had opened the door to the loft. But who –?

Suddenly, there were words echoing in her head.

Do you think Father Christmas might come anyway? . . . If you want to catch him, you'll have to get up on the roof and wave.

But no, that was nonsense! Even Becky couldn't be as stupid as *that*!

All the same, her heart began to thud unpleasantly. For a second she was tempted to get back into bed and go to sleep – to pretend the whole thing had nothing to do with her.

Then she thought what trouble there would be if anyone else discovered Becky up there, and heard who'd told her to go. Quickly and quietly, she padded next door into Paul's room and shook him awake.

At first he was scornful. "Don't be stupid, Imo! She *can't* have got into the loft."

"She *can*!" Imogen hissed. "The bookcase is almost as tall as the ceiling. You've got to come and help me look! And bring your torch."

Paul snuggled deeper into bed. "I don't see why *we* need to bother."

"Suppose she tells Henry what I said? We're bound to get blamed. We always do."

Paul looked sulky. "They can't blame me. *I* didn't tell her to climb up there."

"But you knew all about it," Imogen said spitefully. "And I'll tell them, if you don't come and help me."

Paul pulled a face, but he knew it wasn't just a threat. Grumbling and muttering, he slipped out of bed and pulled on his dressing gown. The two of them crept back into Imogen's room.

It wasn't easy, climbing up the bookshelves. The bookcase was very old and solid, but both of them were terrified it would tip forward and send them crashing to the floor.

43

"I don't see how Becky *could* have got up here," hissed Paul. "She'd have been scared stiff."

"She was asleep, that's how," Imogen said bitterly. "She always has things easy. Oh, do hold the top *steady*!"

Panting and gasping, they scrambled into the loft, and Paul switched on his torch. Quickly, he flashed it over the heaps of boxes and old furniture stacked round the walls.

"There you are! I *told* you she wasn't up here."

But Imogen had been up in the loft before. She pointed at the ceiling, over on the far side. "Look! Where that chest of drawers is."

There was a big rooflight just above the chest of drawers. And it was open.

"She can't be through there!" Paul said, quickly. "It doesn't go anywhere. Only –"

Imogen gritted her teeth. "Only on to the roof."

She was so angry that she wanted to yell and throw things around. Stupid, mean, *selfish* Becky! What right did *she* have to get upset and sleepwalk?

But there was no point in yelling yet. First they had to steer Becky back to bed. Then they could think of a revenge.

"I'll take a look up there." Imogen scrambled on to the chest of drawers and wriggled her head out through the window opening.

And there was Becky.

She was sitting right up on the ridge of the roof, quite still in the moonlight. The red-and-white striped sock was clutched in her hand, and her eyes were wide and vague.

"Well?" said Paul impatiently, from inside the loft. "What can you see?"

"She's there all right." Imogen swallowed. "Fast asleep. We'll have to go and get her."

Paul gave a funny little squeak. "But – don't you think we ought to fetch Mum and Henry?"

"And ask for trouble?" Imogen said scornfully.

"But – it's dangerous!"

Imogen looked at Becky, perched high above the garden. She was very close, so close that they could almost have reached out and touched her.

Imogen looked the other way, at the slope of the roof. On that side of the house it swooped down over the extension, almost to ground level. A very long, slippery slide.

"It's all right," she said stubbornly. "If Becky can do it, so can we."

She hoisted herself up till she was sitting in the open window space. Then, taking a deep breath, she hauled herself to her feet and grabbed at the roof.

A tile slid away under her hands and clattered all the way down, bouncing on the gutter and disappearing into the laurel bushes.

"What was that?" hissed Paul.

"Nothing!" snapped Imogen. She could see how to do it now, and she didn't want Paul backing out because he was nervous.

Putting one foot on the side hinge of the roof light, she scrambled on to the top of the frame and grabbed at the summit of the roof. A second later, she was sitting behind Becky, trying not to look down.

"Come on, Paul!" she hissed. "Don't chicken out."

Paul's pale face appeared in the window opening. "Isn't it better if I stay down here? To help her in."

"No it isn't!" snapped Imogen. She wanted him up there with her, taking his chance. "I'll tell you how to climb. It's really simple."

He seemed to take for ever pulling himself up, and when he finally reached the ridge he was exhausted and grumbling.

"OK, brains. What do we do now we're up here? She's not exactly taking any notice of us, is she?"

He was right. Becky was between them, not reacting at all as they talked across her. She sat very still, with her face turned up to the sky and the striped sock wound round her right hand.

"We'd better not wake her," Imogen said. "If she stands up, she'll fall right off the roof. If we turn her round, so she's lying against the slope of the roof, one of us can hold her while the other one goes down to catch her feet and put them on the window frame."

"That's what I *said*. I *told* you I didn't need to climb up here –"

"Yes you did! You're not listening –"

"You just wanted me here because you're scared –"

It might have exploded into a full-blown quarrel, but at that moment Becky gave a great cry and turned round, holding out her hand.

"I'M HERE!"

Paul almost fell off the roof. "What on earth –?"

"She's dreaming, you idiot! Quick, grab hold of her arms!"

But Becky had already jumped to her feet. Standing on the very summit of the ridge, she was stretching out, as though she were trying to reach something just ahead of her.

Paul closed his eyes and started to wail. "Oh, no! Oh, no! I can't bear it! We're all going to fall –"

"Don't be such a puking little *coward*! Why don't you help me instead of sitting there snivelling?"

Imogen grabbed at his arm, dragging it upwards so that he had to get to his feet or slip over sideways. But he went on wailing.

"Look at Becky! She's watching something! There's something coming!"

"It's a *dream*, you idiot!" Imogen was beginning to feel desperate. "Shut up or someone'll hear us!"

"But there's something –"

"How can there be anything coming? We're up on the roof!" Imogen scowled at him and caught hold of Becky's left shoulder. "Get her on the other side. We can lift her off her feet and lower her over the edge. Then I'll hold on to her while –".

She never finished the sentence.

All at once, out of nowhere, a great rushing sound whirled towards them, and they were hit by a blast of wind that almost knocked them off the roof.

Thick shadows swept in, blocking out the moonlight. Imogen ducked sideways, dragging Becky off her feet and pulling Paul with her.

"Hold on tight!" she hissed.

"I told you –"

Paul's voice was swallowed in a thunder of wild galloping. Suddenly, all around them, the air exploded in chaos. Clattering hoofs thundered past, clashing against the chimneys and striding out into empty air. And something skimmed overhead, so close that it brushed Imogen's neck and grazed the back of her hand.

It seemed like –

But it couldn't be!

Imogen looked up. For a second, she saw a face peering at her over the edge of the shadows. A huge, impossible face. Rosy cheeks. A great waterfall of white beard. And blue eyes . . .

The eyes were like knives. For that endless second, they held Imogen, piercing right to the centre of her brain. Seeing her, and making her see herself.

Then they had gone, and she was screaming. Screaming, and slithering helplessly down the roof, with one hand twisted into the sleeve of Becky's pyjamas and the other grabbing uselessly at the cold, slippery tiles.

The ambulance came very quickly. Henry had telephoned the instant he saw what had happened, and it was there within ten minutes.

Imogen almost blurted out the whole story while they were waiting. In those first frantic moments, she actually *wanted* to blurt it out. But Henry wouldn't let her talk.

"Keep calm, Imo. Don't worry about anything. Let's find out how you are, first of all."

"But I –"

"There's no hurry, OK? We'll sort it all out later."

By the time the ambulance came, she had pulled herself together. What was the point of getting into trouble when you didn't have to? Much better to wait and see what Becky said.

As they were helping Paul into the ambulance, she caught his eye and put her finger to her lips. *Don't you dare tell . . .* He knew what she meant, all right. *Think I'm daft?* said the look in his eyes.

By the time they reached the hospital, Becky still hadn't said a word. She'd woken up when they hit the ground, but she was dazed, and confused by where she was. And Henry still wasn't worrying about questions.

"But he says she's fine," their mother said, soothingly, as Imogen and Paul waited in the plastering room. "The doctor thinks it's a miracle. All she's got is a few bruises."

Typical, thought Imogen bitterly. *I get a broken leg, Paul gets a broken arm, and dear little Becky gets – nothing.* But she forced a sweet, suffering smile on to her face. "Isn't it lucky she was asleep when she fell?"

Their mother shook her head. "It might have been better if you'd woken Henry and me."

"But we didn't dare leave her," cooed Imogen. "Did we, Paul?"

He shook his head. "We could see she was just about to fall."

Imogen was still worried about what Becky might say, but she crossed her fingers behind her back and hoped for the best.

And it seemed as though they were going to be in luck. When they all met up again in the hospital waiting room, Becky flung herself at them both.

"You're wonderful! You're darlings! It's all my fault you're hurt!"

Paul grinned, smugly, but Imogen managed to look very solemn. "What were you *doing* on the roof, Spicks?"

"I – I don't know. I must have been sleepwalking, I suppose. But I've never got up on the roof before."

"And you'll never get up there again," Henry said grimly. "The moment we're home, I'm going to move those bookshelves out of your bedroom."

He led the way to the car, and Becky snuggled into the back, next to Paul. She kept looking up at him, with big, awed eyes.

"You came up on the roof," she whispered. "Just to save me. You're really *brave*!"

"It was nothing," Paul said, grandly. "Forget it."

Becky looked adoring. "Oh, I won't. *I won't.*"

Too right you won't, thought Imogen. She settled more comfortably into the front seat and began to plan the future. If Becky felt grateful to them – and guilty, for making them climb up on to the roof – she could be made to do all kinds of things.

And Henry would have to be more forgiving too. Because

51

it was his darling little girl who had broken their bones. Really, everything had worked out very well indeed. Worth a few weeks in plaster.

And no one would ever know what had *really* happened.

As they pulled into the drive, Henry glanced up at the house. "Look at that! We were in such a hurry when we followed the ambulance, we left the lights on. They must have been blazing away all day. What a waste of money!"

Still as mean as ever, thought Imogen. Well, she had plans for changing all that, now that Henry felt guilty. He was going to spend and spend and *spend*! She opened the car door and levered herself out on the hospital crutches.

"Let's get inside. I'm *starving*."

Her mother laughed. "Well, you've got your Christmas dinner to come. It should be ready in two or three hours."

She slid her key into the lock, flung the door wide open – and stopped dead.

"What's the matter?" Imogen said, hobbling towards her. "If you don't hurry up and turn the oven on, the turkey won't be cooked until midnight."

Henry came up behind them. "Something wrong?"

Imogen's mother didn't answer. She just pointed across the hall and into the sitting room. "Look!"

There, on the right of the fireplace, was a sock hanging on a nail. A long red-and-white football sock.

It was stretched as wide as it could go, bulging with lumps and angles. And sticking out of the top was a golden-curled, blue-eyed doll with a sweet pink face. She wore a silver cat charm round her neck and carried a bundle of pink writing paper tucked under one arm.

"Oh!" said Becky. "*Oh*! But who –?"

She started forward, her face lit up with delight. But Imogen didn't bother to watch her. She and Paul were staring with horrified eyes at the other side of the fireplace.

There were socks hanging there too, but they weren't red-and-white football socks. They were grubby, tattered relics from the bottom of the mending basket. And through the holes in the toes, a thin stream of grey trickled steadily on to the hearth stones.

Dust and ashes.

For a second, Imogen almost blacked out. The room swirled around her and she couldn't see anything except a huge face, and a pair of piercing blue eyes.

I didn't – I didn't mean –

But she couldn't say a word. And even through the rushing in her ears, she could hear Paul's babbling, panic-stricken voice:

"It was all Imogen's fault –"

CHRISTMAS GAME

Susan Price

re you going to be all right?" June said.

"Yes Mum." David wished she would just go.

"And you know where I'm going to be?"

He folded his arms and leaned on the banister. "Just across the road at number 42."

"I wrote down their number, didn't I? By the 'phone. If anything's wrong, just ring or come and fetch me. You don't mind me going, do you?"

"No, Mum."

"I wish you could come as well – it seems a shame you being stuck here – but they haven't invited any children, so that's –"

"Mum, if they'd invited me, you couldn't go. Who'd stay with Kenny?"

"That's true." She paused a moment and then started up again. "I wouldn't go, but –" David sighed, and tipped back his head, closing his eyes. "You're too old, aren't you, to care about Christmas Eve? And Kenny's in bed, and it was so kind of them to ask me. You *don't* mind, do you?"

Eyes closed, head leaning against the stair-rail, he said, "Just *go!*"

"I wonder if I should go and check on Kenny?"

She set one foot on the bottom stair, and David's head snapped down. "No! You might wake him up and he's been a pest all day!"

"He's excited, David. It's Christmas Eve, and he's only little."

"He didn't have to draw in my book."

"Oh, your teacher'll understand. Don't make such a fuss."

David pushed himself away from the banister, turned and went back into the living-room. Kenny had drawn bright crayon pictures of Santa Claus and his reindeer across four pages of his history book. His teacher would *not* understand. Four pages of his exercise book that he couldn't use, and books had to last the whole year. It wasn't even as if he got on well with his history teacher. It would be, "You should look after your things better, Rose. Then you wouldn't have to make excuses." His mother was always the same. Kenny was let off, no matter what he did. David always had to stop making a fuss.

He had work to do, but he couldn't settle to it until he knew his mother was out of the house, and he hadn't heard the front door slam yet. She'd probably gone upstairs to check on darling Kenny. He sat in an armchair by the fire, on the edge of the seat, waiting, with gritted teeth, for her to get off out.

Timmy got up from the hearth-rug with a grunt, reared up, and put warm, hard paws on David's knees. Without thinking, David's hand went to Timmy's head – but then he pushed the dog away. Timmy wasn't his. He belonged to the next-door neighbours, who had gone away to Portugal for Christmas and dumped the snappy little cake-hound on the Roses. Mrs Rose couldn't say 'no', and David was stuck with having to take the thing for walks. For days now he'd been resisting the little terrier's wagging tail and white grin. There was no point in getting fond of him. He'd go back to his owners in a few days.

He heard the front door slam as his mother left for her party at last, and he grimaced. He was glad for her. She didn't get out much, and she'd been so obviously pleased at being invited that she'd seemed younger than him. She'd come and shown him how she looked in her best frock, with her face made up and her hair styled, and had blushed and been embarrassed when he'd said she looked nice. He'd been telling the truth when he'd said that he didn't mind her going to the party, even though he had to stay at home and do school work. It was just the way she went on and on and kept fussing about Kenny that irritated him. Kenny had put out a mince-pie and a glass of sherry for Santa Claus, he'd hung up his stocking, and he'd gone off to bed quite happy, after a day of making a nuisance of himself. There'd been no need to check on him half a dozen times.

He got up and went back to the table, where his books were spread out. Economics. Who wanted to be doing economics on Christmas Eve? He slumped in his chair and looked across at the tree in the corner, draped with tinsel and hung with globes. The mantelpiece was cluttered with cards, and at the other end of the table stood the sherry and mince-pie for Santa Claus, all set out very elegantly. Kenny had used one of his mother's best china plates and one of her best glasses, and it was all standing on an embroidered tray cloth. Still it didn't seem like Christmas Eve to David – just another day, with homework to be done.

He picked up his pen and made himself write another sentence in his essay. Then he drank the sherry, ate the mince-pie, and made himself look through some pages of text books. Timmy stretched and sighed on the hearth.

David took an hour off to watch television, dragged

himself back to his books and managed to write another paragraph and then, exhausted, lay on his back on the floor, staring at the Christmas tree until the spangles and brightness blurred in his eyes. The evening crawled by: nine o'clock, ten, eleven. His mother still didn't come home. It must be a good party.

It was getting on for midnight when the door of the room opened, and he looked up, expecting his mother, though he hadn't heard her key in the lock. No one came in, but he was looking too high. As the door continued to open, he looked lower down, and saw Kenny in his pyjamas.

"What are you doing out of bed?"

"Santa Claus hasn't been!" Kenny said. "There's no presents."

It irritated David that Kenny could still believe in Santa Claus. "It isn't morning yet, dope! Get back to bed."

"It is morning. I've been asleep."

David got up from the table. "Just because you've been asleep doesn't mean it's morning. Bed!"

Kenny caught sight of the empty plate and glass, and his mouth and eyes opened wide. "He *has* been! He ate his pie!"

"I ate it," David said. "You've got to go back to bed."

Kenny was shocked and outraged. "You ate Santa Claus' pie!"

"If you don't go back to bed, Santa Claus won't come here

59

at all. Look. If I let you put out another pie and another glass, will you go to bed then?"

Kenny stuck his fingers in his mouth, stared at David, and made an 'um' noise, which might have been agreement, so David went into the kitchen to fetch the tin of mince-pies and the bottle of sherry.

Kenny left off stroking Timmy and cried, "I want to do it!" as soon as David came into the room.

"Okay." David put the tin and bottle on the table, and dragged a chair close. He lifted Kenny up onto the chair, and opened the tin for him. Carefully, as if it was an enormously difficult and important operation, Kenny took a pie from the tin and placed it in the very centre of the china plate. He sucked the sugar off his fingers. "Now the wine," he said.

"Give me a chance." David replaced the lid on the tin, and unscrewed the top of the bottle. "Let me help you hold it." He supported the weight of the bottle while Kenny grasped its neck and guided the mouth more or less over the glass. Brown sherry splashed out. "Careful!" David said, but some sherry splashed on the white tray cloth anyway. Kenny didn't seem to notice, and grinned with pride as David put the top back on the bottle.

"Can I have a pie?"

"If you take it to bed with you," David said.

"Give me a pie!"

David tugged the lid off the tin again, and allowed Kenny to take a pie. "Now, bed."

Kenny seated himself on the chair, and bit into the pie. "I want to stop up and see Santa Claus come."

"You promised you'd go to bed!"

"Didn't," Kenny said.

"Mum put you to bed. She'll be mad if she comes home and finds you up."

"Don't care," Kenny said.

"You will."

"Shan't!" Kenny said. He stuffed the last of the pie into his mouth and jumped down from the chair, heading for Timmy on the hearth.

"Oh, no!" David said, and grabbed him. Let him start playing with the dog, and there'd be no getting him to bed. Kenny immediately began to shriek with fury, screams that made David wince. He threw himself down on the carpet, letting his whole weight drag on David's arms. "I'll tell Mum, I'll tell Mum!" the child cried.

"Tell her what?" It was amazing how heavy Kenny could make himself, and how many arms and legs he seemed to have to kick and punch with.

"I'll tell her you hit me and were cruel to me!"

And their mother would probably believe him. David's

shoe slipped on the carpet, and he fell, banging his elbow hard on the floor. Kenny landed on top of him, and that hurt too. And the dog, Timmy, came dancing round them, barking. David lost his temper.

"All right! Stay up! You'll fall asleep on the floor before I put you to bed!"

"Shan't!" said Kenny, all tears gone, and crawled off David and over to the hearth, all smiles and ready to play with Timmy.

Kenny's smugness was infuriating. The brat had got his own way again. "Stay up until Santa Claus comes!" David said. "You'll be sorry. You'll wish you hadn't."

"Shan't!" Kenny said.

David picked himself up and found himself standing close by the tree. A little figure of Santa Claus, with a red coat of cardboard and a white beard of cotton wool, hung from a branch. He pulled it from the tree, sending a shower of rustling, dry needles down to the carpet, and jingling the globes together. His anger extended to Santa Claus. He'd always been irritated by that fat old, smirking, red-faced boozy chimney-climber.

"You think it's Santa Claus who's going to come, don't you? A nice kind old man with toys in a sack. But it won't be. Oh, no!"

"Who will it be, then?" Kenny asked.

"Father Christmas, that's who."

Kenny stared at him for a moment but then looked away and stroked Timmy. "Same thing."

"No," David said. "No. Not the same thing. That's 'Santa Claus'." He threw the tree ornament down by Kenny and stepped over him and the dog to take a card from the mantelpiece. "*That's* Father Christmas."

The picture on the card wasn't the usual bright Christmassy card picture. It showed a gloomy room with a laughing giant seated at its centre on a heap of food – pies and cakes and Christmas puddings and little barrels. There were dead animals too: hares, little pigs and pheasants. The giant's bare feet rested among them. In one hand he held up a burning stick, and in the other a large cup from which wine was spilling. His long robe was of dark green, trimmed with white fur. He had a beard, but it was a dark one, and long dark hair fell to his shoulders. His head was crowned by a wreath of green holly-leaves and red berries.

"That's not Father Christmas," Kenny said. "Where's his sack? Santa Claus' coat is red, not green. And his beard's white."

"That shows how little you know," David said. "Father Christmas and Santa Claus aren't the same thing. Completely different."

"Not," Kenny said, but David could see he wasn't sure of

himself. After a whole day of the little pest making his life difficult, that was something.

"Father Christmas came first," David said. "Santa Claus is nothing – he was invented for a Coca-Cola advert not so long ago – only about sixty years ago."

"That's a long time," Kenny said.

"It is to *you*, because you're only six –"

"Nearly seven!"

"Only six. So you know nothing. Santa Claus and his red coat and his white beard – that's just an advert. Father Christmas is much older. Ever so old." David made his voice as sinister as he could. "He was old before people ever heard of Jesus and started having Christmas."

"Why's he called Father Christmas then?" Kenny asked.

"He wasn't always. He was only called that *after* people started believing in Jesus and having Christmas. Before that he was called –" he groped into his memory of the newspaper article he'd read the day before, one of those seasonal pieces about Christmas customs. "– called *Wotan*."

He had Kenny's full attention now. "Wotan?"

"Wotan, God of the Dead!" David said.

"Dead?" Kenny almost choked. He was afraid of ghosts and skeletons and didn't like talk of the dead.

"Oh, he had his good side –" David paused. He hadn't read the article carefully, and it hadn't made that much sense. "He brought good luck to some people. But he wasn't all goody-goody. He was God of the Dead! He lived underground with the dead, and at night, at dark of night –"

"Shut up!" Kenny said. "You shouldn't say things like this; you'll frighten me!"

"Chicken!" David said. "Listen. At deep dark of night, when the wind's howling –"

"I'll tell Mum you frightened me!"

"Oh, like I hit you and was cruel to you? Wotan comes riding through the dark, on his wild steed, with his ravening dogs, their eyes all glowing like fires –"

"Shut up!" Kenny said, trembling into tears, and struck out at him.

David caught his hand and held it. He'd keep it up until the little brat was crying properly, he thought, and then leave off. It'd teach the little pest not to be such a pain.

"You know what he hunts? You know what Wotan hunts? Ghosts. All the lost souls who've died that year, all wailing and sobbing as they run from Wotan and his headless hounds that have flames burning where their heads should be!"

Kenny was crying outright now, snivelling, his small frame shaking as David held him between his hands.

"And if you stay up to see Father Christmas come, like a naughty little boy, *that's* who'll come – the *real* Father

Christmas, Wotan! He'll come, looking for souls, for your soul!"

"He won't – he won't, will he, David? He won't!" He tried to move forward, into his brother's arms, looking for comfort, but David pushed him away and stepped away from him, leaving him crying in the middle of the room. David knew he should stop it now – but when he thought of the drawings in his history book and the embarrassment they were going to cause him, of the carefully made model aeroplanes that Kenny had broken, and all the general annoyance that Kenny had given him, he decided that Kenny should suffer a bit longer.

"Do you want to go to bed now – on your own?" he asked. Kenny shook his head, wailing, tears running down his face. "Do you want to stop up and wait for Wotan to come, then?" Again, Kenny sobbed. "I'm going to call Wotan," David said. "I know a magic spell. I'm going to say the spell and make Wotan come here."

"No, David! Don't, David! Don't!"

Kenny ran after him as he darted across the room and took down a red-berried branch of holly from a vase on the mantelpiece.

"By this holly," David said, spinning to avoid Kenny's clutching hands, "King of the Wood, Ever-Green, I summon you, Wotan, Lord of the Dead!"

"David!" Timmy had begun to leap about them both and bark.

David danced over to the decoration on the shelves, and took up a sprig of mistletoe. "By this mistletoe, white as the midnight moon, white as ghosts, white as corpses, by this holly, red as blood, I summon you, Wotan, Hunter of Souls!"

Timmy stopped leaping, sat, and howled – a nice touch that David couldn't have timed better.

"By this tree, by this dead but ever-green tree, Wotan, Hunter of Souls, Lord of the Dead, I summon you!"

Kenny was no longer chasing him. He was sitting on the floor in the middle of the room, sobbing.

"Wotan! Come! Wotan! Come! Wotan –!" David could hardly speak for laughing. The shrillness of Timmy's howls and Kenny's wails made it all seem funnier. It was only when one wail rose high, high, higher than a dog's howl or a little boy's sobbing, that he broke off his chanting and his laughing and listened.

There was a sound – above and beside the sounds of Kenny and Timmy – a keening that was quite mindless, that was afraid and frightening. It made him want to run.

Between one blink and another he found that the lights had gone out. A power-failure? And cold! It was so cold.

His eyes were looking into darkness and distance – there

were no walls to stop his gaze. That cold was no draught, but the wind blowing out of miles distant, carrying the chill and rasp of winter. There was the Christmas tree – but, beyond it, another tree, and another, black shapes in the darkness that had suddenly come. And still that sound, that rising and falling, shapeless, gabbling of fear –

"David!" Kenny fell against him, and David clutched at him, finding his small hand and holding it tight.

"It's all right, Kenny." He heard his own voice choking. "Don't worry. It's all right."

They were outside. He grasped that much. There was the sky, black and darkest blue, with icy stars suddenly gleaming between the clouds. There was the dark mass of the land around them, and the cold wind scratching at them, and the sound of the wind in the trees, like sighs, like rain, and above that, the sound of crying, of wailing and crying out.

David twisted his body and neck, looking for the house. Find the house, get Kenny back inside and lock the door. But there were no houses. He peered into the darkness, seeing only the shaggy blackness of trees. No lights, except the flash of stars; no sounds of cars, only the sound of the wind shuddering through the trees, and that wailing.

The wailing was louder. Clutching at Kenny, pushing him behind his back, David turned to face it. There was movement against the sky; he saw a wave of arms, a turn of heads,

68

and then he saw them pouring across the sky and down from it – people running. Not looking back, but staring before them and running. Their mouths were open and they wailed, but they had no message, no meaning, no language – it was only terror that made them moan.

And behind them – behind them came the Hunt. The flickering, leaping light that touched the clouds, and lit the trees moment by moment, came from the flames that were the heads of sprinting hounds. And then came riders, but not on horses. No horse ever carried on its head those towering branches, black against the sky. Stags – the hunt were mounted on black stags.

Clamping Kenny's hand in his, David ran. The little boy trailed out behind him, heavy and dragging. Turning, David heaved him up into his arms, and then tried to run again. There was no sense in it. He could not be here, trying to run with weighted legs and clogging heart, in this dark and cold, but here he was. He had to keep hold of Kenny. Past them went running shapes, moaning and sobbing. None of the runners looked round, none of them cared for anything but to run, and their cries were not cries for help, but cries of misery. We can't be here, with them, David thought – but they were, they were, and the only thing was to run, because of what was behind.

The shrieks on every side were louder, more piercing,

more desperate, and the creatures – whatever, whoever they were – turned in every direction, and struck out against those near them. Twisting his head, David saw a black bulk rising above him, a branching tree seemingly growing from its head, a rolling red eye – and above that, riding it, another black shape. And this black shape reached –

David squealed and turned from it, and felt his heart swell as he tried to run yet faster – and then the weight was gone from his arms. Kenny was gone. Flinging his arms wide, he turned again, and saw the black shape rearing above him, and a sudden wavering light showed him Kenny's shape, slung as if dead, slung like a water-bottle on a saddle-bow. He yelled and reached for Kenny, but the black shape lunged forward and was gone, the hunt passed him by, streaming into the darkness after the wailing of its prey.

David stood in darkness and falling silence, and then clutched at his head, feeling madness swelling there. He looked round for safety, but there was none – and where could he go without Kenny? He ran on, stumbling on rough ground, twisting his ankles, bruising and jarring himself as he fell full length, but getting up and running forward again, after the hunt and the fading wails of the hunted.

All sounds of the hunt left him, and he was in darkness – the full, dense darkness of the unlit countryside, where no step can be taken in certainty. The only sound was the soughing and sighing of wind in unseen trees. He stopped, and at least knew that he wouldn't fall – but how long could he stand there? Whichever way he turned, there was no light; and everything was so strange, how did he know there would ever be light again? "What's happened?" he said. He meant to shout it, but was afraid of what might hear, and whispered instead.

Struggling on, he fell into thorns, and panicked as he fought out of them, scratching his arms and face. He struck his head on hard branches, tumbled and banged his knees and grazed his hands, and was miserable.

But ahead he saw a faint glow in the sky – a firelight glow, warming and fading with the flickering of the flames. Feeling relief and joy, he made towards it, and was dazzled by it, so that he fell and banged himself on trees more often. Still, he got closer and saw fountains of sparks spring up into the darkness, and even felt the warmth blow towards him on the wind.

He reached the top of a rise and smelt the wood smoke, heard the crackling of flames as they gnawed, saw below him, in a sheltered hollow, the red and yellow jumping of the fire. Around it were black shapes, moving, shouting, even singing. The huntsmen.

He made his way around the hollow, keeping at a distance from the fire, and feeling all the colder now he was near warmth. He saw the leader of the hunt, enthroned. A big, broad man, dressed in green. He wore a crown of green and red holly on his dark hair. His throne was the catch of the hunt, piled high; deer, birds, foxes, hares – and men, women and children. His dogs were gathered round him, the Yell-hounds, some with heads and gaping, toothed mouths; some with no heads but burning flames.

David went down into the hollow and towards the throne of game. He was afraid. He limped as he went, and felt blood trickling down his legs and the wind thrashing his disordered hair about his face.

The Huntsman turned to watch him as he approached, the flaring, wind-blown fire lighting his face. He had only one eye.

By the Huntsman's foot, in a soft heap, lay Kenny. David tried to go forward to touch him, but the hounds stirred, bristled and growled. Most of all he was afraid of the ones with flames for heads.

His foot twisted on some unevenness, and he fell, bashing his knees again. The hounds twitched and growled, and the flame-heads lunged towards him. He shrank back from the lick of heat. But the hounds looked to their master, and though they groaned with eagerness to reach him, and twitched and shifted their haunches, they stayed in place.

Kenny's face was turned towards him, lying as David had

so often seen him lie on his pillow, but now with his cheek to the cold ground. His lips and chin were stained with a darkness, as if he'd been eating chocolate or blackberries. Then David saw that the darkness had pooled on the ground, and when a hound put down its muzzle and licked at it, he knew it was blood. He began to shake and sob.

"It doesn't make sense," he said. "It doesn't make sense." Yet the hard ground that had cut his knees was real. The cold he felt clenched around him was real.

Something moved in the firelit shadows, and he flinched. It was the Huntsman. Leaning down from his throne, the holly berries of his crown blazing red as they caught the light of the fire, he spread his hand before David as if to make him look at it. His broad, thick hand cupped and caressed a small sapling that grew from the ground at the base of his throne. A bare stick, leafless, it was enduring through the winter, waiting for the warm times to come again.

David looked from the sapling to the Huntsman's face, with its one gleaming eye, and its one sagging lid hanging over a dark socket. When he looked back at the sapling again, he saw the Huntsman's hand tighten around it. He pulled, and the sapling came from the ground. The Huntsman was strong – his pull broke even that frozen earth – and something was rising from the soil, dragged by the sapling's roots. David leaned closer and saw that it was a skull. The sapling's roots had crept deep in the empty eye sockets of a skull.

"Death is life," said the Huntsman. "*That* is the sense."

"But he's only little – and I didn't mean it! He's my little brother –"

The Huntsman reached down and lifted Kenny by the scruff of the neck, holding him up as a poacher might hold a dead rabbit, a piece of game.

"You wish I should take another in his stead?" The Huntsman leaned towards David, yellow teeth grinning through the darkness of his beard, his blind socket seeming to peer at him. "Which other should I take? You?"

David trembled where he knelt. *No* was his only thought, but he knew that if the Huntsman held his silence long enough, he would say yes, because it was impossible to give up Kenny.

The Huntsman was still grinning. "Promise me the life of the first to greet you on your return."

"My – my return?"

The Huntsman held Kenny dangling. "A life for a life. In the stead of this child, I shall take the first to greet you on your return. Do you agree, freely?"

"The first –" David's mind groped for meaning, and suddenly saw a clear picture. The little dog, Timmy,

74

rushing at him, yapping wildly, as he had every day since he'd been with them. "Yes! I agree – yes!"

The Huntsman stood and dangled Kenny into his arms. David hugged Kenny tightly to him, gladly taking his weight. Kenny was warm, and turned his head against David's shoulder, wiping blood on to his jumper from nothing worse than a bleeding nose.

The Huntsman stepped to the fire, and took up a burning branch. The light, golden and flaring, fell over his dark hair and scarlet and green crown, filled his empty socket with blackness, turned the folds of his green robe the colour of leaves in summer. "The first to greet you," he said.

David's gaze was stopped short by a wall. And there was the Christmas tree, closed in by the walls of the room, its plastic icicles shimmering in the electric lamplight. The warmth of the house pressed so close around him that his chilled flesh felt suddenly as hard as stone.

Chilled! He *had* been cold. And Kenny, straining his arms with his weight, had a bloodied face; and he could feel the soreness of his cut knees, feel water trickling down his neck from his wet hair. It was real, and there was a bargain to be kept. Where was the dog?

He stooped to lay his sleeping brother on the settee, and as he was freeing his arm from beneath the little boy, his mother's voice said, "Hello! Where have you been?"

David straightened and turned, and no one was behind him. He had been mistaken; he had heard nothing. But the door to the hall was open now, when before it had been closed – and through it came Timmy, with his hair hanging in his eyes, and his little stump of a tail wagging.

Feeling stiff-jointed and dazed, David left Kenny sleeping and went out into the hall and along the passage into the kitchen. His heart lurched as he saw someone move. His sight cleared, and he recognised his mother's back as she lit the gas-ring, the soft loose folds of her party frock billowing about her.

David couldn't speak. He had heard his mother's voice. His mother had been the first to greet him.

She turned, looked at him, and smiled. "Want a tea or coffee?" David couldn't answer. He watched as his mother spun round to reach the kettle, watched as her loose sleeve brushed through the flames and became flame itself.

His mother's first yell was of astonishment rather than fear. The kettle went flying into the sink with a loud, ringing clang. She flapped her arm, trying to knock the flames out, and they flared higher up her sleeve and caught her hair.

Frozen, David watched his mother beat at her own head, watched the loose dress swirl with her movement, and snatch flames for itself.

"Help me! Help me!"

David ran forward and, astonished by the heat, fell back a step. He couldn't reach the sink and the water for the flames burning on his mother. And now she was screaming shattering screams that seemed to hit David like blows and leave him as shaken.

A bottle of milk stood on the table. He snatched it up and threw it over his mother. Most of it missed.

The burning woman fell away from the sink. David jumped forward, turned on the taps and snatched a large jug from the draining board, but – oh God! While the jug was filling, his mother was burning.

She'd fallen to the floor and was rolling wildly, and some of the flames were out. David flung the water at her and ran around the table, still carrying the jug. He shoved past something in the doorway. As he reached the 'phone he realised that the something had been a silent, staring Kenny. He dialled 999.

Christmas Day dawned and David lay, hugging Kenny, in a strange bed in a strange room in a neighbour's house, listening to the wind rising. It thrummed in the roof-space; it buffeted the windows; it reached into the house and rattled the cupboard doors. And through it he heard, rising higher, that soughing and sighing of a forest cut down long ago, a sound that could have been rain or distant running. He heard a bang at the window that could have been a blow from a fist; a wail that could have been his mother's voice, and then the keening – a mindless, terrified crying – ran away, ran before what chased it.

Downstairs the telephone rang, with the news he knew was coming.

SQUATTERS

Jill Bennett

andra Biggs stared at herself in the bathroom mirror.

It was Friday night five days before Christmas and the parties had begun. Sandra (Sandy – she hated Sandra, it made her feel all scratchy) had been planning her outfit for days. She'd bought a new lipstick and blusher to match and was going to do her hair like the model on the cover of *Top Girl*. With her black leggings and new cerise and lime green top, she'd show them!

So there she was, all decked out in her new outfit, and it hadn't made a particle of difference.

Her pale face wasn't really improved by the fashionable brownish lipstick, and the blusher on her round cheeks stood out in artificial triangles. She had pulled her light brown frizzy hair into a ponytail on the side of her head and, frankly, she knew she looked silly.

She was fourteen, plump, and a serious spot was about to erupt on the side of her nose.

"Dracula's grandmother!" Sandy shouted at herself to keep the tears at bay.

She flung her hairbrush at the basin. It made an almighty clatter as it bounced out and landed on the floor at her feet.

"Sandra!" Her mother's voice floated up the stairs. "What are you doing up there?"

Sandy didn't reply. She grabbed at a tissue and viciously wiped the make-up off her face. It looked blotchy now, but she didn't care any more.

Smarting and feeling desperate she came heavily down the stairs and reached for her old school anorak. She'd go to the party anyway. Fat old Sandy.

Her mother stood at the sitting room door.

"Here," she demanded. "Where d'you think you're off to?"

"The moon," Sandy said rudely.

"You cheeky little cow," said Sandy's mother, looking at her daughter with that certain smile Sandy dreaded. "You look a mess. Something the cat sicked up, you are. I don't think you should be let out. You never said."

"I don't have to tell you everything." The old empty cavern began to open up inside Sandy when her mother said things like that. Sometimes it grew so deep Sandy thought she'd fall into it and never be seen again.

"Sandra. You come here!" Her stepfather's voice joined in harshly and her mother stood aside to let Sandy take a reluctant step over the sitting room threshold.

A large man rose from the sofa and moved towards her. He had lost most of the hair at the front of his head and wore a thick moustache to compensate. He'd been her stepfather for two years now. Sandy had had time to practise her sullen, silent response to almost everything he said or did. She hated him. She hated her dad too for walking out on them, and quite often she hated her mother for bringing this man into her home.

"Don't you give your mother lip!" He held a can of beer in one hand and wiped his mouth with the other. "You'll do that once too often, my girl."

On the other side of the sofa the TV was showing an early evening game show and a large plate of sandwiches stood on the low table in front of it.

Sandy's glance took it all in. They hadn't offered her any food, but by now she was used to being treated as if she didn't exist. Her mother was completely wrapped up in her new husband.

So why does she bother if I want to go out? she thought. She just wants to make a show of being a mum to impress him. The black cavern inside her stretched wider. Was there a time, Sandy wondered, when her mother had been any different? She glowered at them from under her brows, sullen and silent.

Her stepfather put his free arm over her mother's shoulders and they leaned against one another and stared at her.

Sandy couldn't keep it up. She stared back at each of them in turn.

"I'm off then. Don't bother to wait up."

"You take a step outside that door and you're for it!" her mother said halfheartedly.

Sandy knew she was just keeping up the pressure. Her mother didn't really want her company, they'd only row.

"Yeah." Her stepfather almost sniggered. "You never know what could happen to a little raver like you, Sandra!" His look clearly said that no one, but no one, would even bother molesting her.

The knife struck home and Sandy fought back.

"Well, at least I'm young," she shouted at them. "I've got my life ahead of me, I have. You're just a couple of middle-aged has-beens trying to be twenty. I'm sorry for you, you hear?" She unhooked her shoulder bag from the banister and turned away.

"Come back here, you!" Her mother sprang forward and grabbed her arm. With her other hand she gave Sandy a stinging blow across her cheek. The man leaned forward and held his wife round the waist.

"Steady, Marge. Let the little cow go. What's it to us?"

Sandy held a hand up to her flaming cheek. The rest of her face was white.

"That's it, then." To her surprise she didn't shout. She turned back to the front door and opened it.

Her mother felt unnerved by her unnaturally quiet voice.

"Where're you going now?" she asked, vaguely alarmed.

Sandy looked at her. "As I said," she continued in the same quiet voice, "don't wait up. I'm going somewhere I'll be welcome. You won't have to bother with me again. Ever. All right?"

The chill December air from the street filled the little hall where they were standing and made them all shiver. Sandy stepped through the door and, with infinite care, closed it behind her.

She let out a long breath as her steps took her numbly down the familiar street. When her road joined the High Street she stopped. Her head was still ringing from her mother's blow but it was the slow accumulation of hurts deeper and stronger than that which had finally burst, like an over-filled balloon.

She meant what she said. It wasn't an idle threat. Her parents wouldn't feel threatened anyway. She doubted if they would take it seriously until she hadn't come home by breakfast time, and then what? She couldn't imagine what they'd do. Anyway, that didn't concern her now. She felt quite calm.

She was going to Tony. His last phonecall had been in October. This time he'd given her the address of a new squat he was in. She fumbled in her bag to find the scrap of paper with the address on it.

It was very crumpled and had a wine gum sticking to a corner.

61 Portello Road, Hammersmith.

Popping the wine gum into her mouth she suddenly thought, I haven't got any of my things. But she wasn't going home to get them, not now.

"Right." Sandy headed for the station, thinking as she went. She had eight pounds and a bit of change in her purse. That would cover the ticket to London and also the underground fare. After that Tony would take care of her and tell her what to do.

Tony Biggs, Sandy's older brother, had left home in much the same way as Sandy two years before. He was seventeen then and Sandy twelve.

"Look, Sand," Tony had said to her when he knew he was

going. "There's just not room in the house for him and me."
The rows with their new stepfather had been terrible. Tony
had told her he was going to stay with a friend who had a
room in London, find a job and then get a place of his own.
Although he was five years older than her she'd missed him
sorely. They had clung to each other when their father left
and their mother had begun to lose her grip on things. Sandy
felt adrift and lonely when Tony went and his phonecalls
were few and erratic.

The winter evening settled in with a chill east wind
blowing. London was only three-quarters of an hour away
and as her train sped through the darkness, Sandy felt a
spurt of excitement. She wondered if there would be other
people in Tony's squat. There usually were. Would they
want her? Tony would see she was fine, no problem.

People filled the London platform as Sandy got out. She
bought her favourite choc-bar from a newspaper stand and
asked the woman where the underground was.

"You blind or something?" The woman barely looked at
her.

She was standing by the entrance.

Squashed with masses of others on a huge escalator,
Sandy began to feel afraid.

"It's miles down," she thought.

As she asked her way on to a Hammersmith train she felt

the old black hole coming at her again. In spite of the brightly lit compartment, she shivered.

"Tony, please, please be there," she prayed.

With unsteady hands she tore the wrapper from her choc-bar and took a bite. Its sweetness comforted her so she took another and chewed it hard. The black hole faded a little, but didn't go away.

At last Sandy stood on the edge of the enormous roundabout at the heart of Hammersmith Broadway. People rushed passed her, heads down against the bitter cold. Christmas illuminations floated across the streets in giant snowflakes, the old glass-fronted pubs glowed yellow and hundreds of traffic lights winked at her.

She was terrified.

As a young woman hurried along with a pushchair, Sandy took a chance and stopped her. She held out her piece of paper, forbidding her teeth to chatter in the icy wind.

"Please, can you tell me where this is?"

The young woman squinted at the paper under the spill of a street light. She looked at Sandy kindly.

"It's not that far, love," she told her. "I'm going that way. Come with me."

They left the bustle and light of the centre and turned into a side street. Sandy lost count of the times they turned corners; one terraced street looked just like another.

"This is Portello Road," the woman said. "Nearly there, love. G'night," and with a quick wave, she hurried away.

Alone again, Sandy stood at the top of the street. The houses in the terrace looked squashed together, shoulder to shoulder in the murky yellow street lighting.

She started walking. There was no one about.

The first houses in the street were lived in and had curtains in their windows. After about Number 40 things began to change. These houses looked uncared for and dilapidated. Some had large cracks in their stucco façades, revealing the old bricks, and others had broken and boarded windows.

Number 61 was barely visible on a dirty fanlight above a chipped front door.

Sandy stared at the house in disbelief. This couldn't be it. The downstairs windows were roughly boarded up with all manner of wooden bits nailed across them. Scrunched up newspapers filled in the gaps and the broken glass panes had many jagged edges. There was not a light to be seen.

She negotiated the crumbling steps to the door. An old electric bell hung on a ragged flex to one side of it, and there was a scar where there had once been a knocker. Sandy tapped timidly.

The sound disappeared into the noises of the city.

In desperation and with a feeling that she had nothing to

lose, she picked up a stray piece of wood and belaboured the door with it. She did this for some time.

Eventually she stopped for breath and listened.

"Oi! You there. Stop that!" A voice came from somewhere above.

Sandy stepped backwards down the steps to get a view of the upper windows.

A sash window on the floor above had been flung open. The room behind the window was as dark as the street but Sandy made out the shape of a head and shoulders leaning out.

"What're you trying to do, man? Be a one-girl demolition squad?"

Sandy peered up. Her heart nearly stopped altogether. A man's black face was staring down at her, hung about with dreadlocks. He looked fearsome.

She nearly ran. Only the realisation that there was nowhere else to go kept her standing there.

"Is Tony Biggs there?" she shouted back to keep her voice from trembling.

The voice from the window lowered in volume.

"Who wants him?"

"Sandy. His sister."

"His what?"

"I'm his sister."

"Wait there." The head and dreadlocks disappeared. Sandy could hear faint sounds in the house, getting nearer. She held her breath. He hadn't said Tony wasn't there, that was something.

With a creak and shove the front door jerked open a little way. An arm came out and grabbed Sandy by the hand and she was yanked through it to stand in pitch blackness on the other side. It was no warmer there.

The arm that yanked her through was now sliding a large bolt of wood across the door. Then she felt her hand grabbed again and she was propelled up a flight of rickety stairs that creaked under their combined weight.

At the top of the stairs another door was opened and she was unceremoniously jerked into a front bedroom. Or rather, what was meant to be a bedroom when it was built some hundred years ago. Now it obviously served many purposes.

Without turning round, she said, "Where's Tony, then?"

"How do I know?" The figure behind her spoke. "How do I know you're Tony's real sister and not a spy from the council?"

This thought was so bizarre that Sandy almost snorted. She turned to stare and saw a young black man scowling at her suspiciously. He was much taller than her and dressed in an assortment of tattered clothes. There was an air of menace about him.

"Do I look like a spy?" she said helplessly.

She looked cold and bedraggled and she was consumed with hunger. The energy that had filled her and given her the power to get this far was gone. She didn't want all this. She wanted her brother, and in spite of biting it hard her lip quivered.

The menace softened. "Heeey! You look like ol' Tone, an' all!" The young man's voice was pleasant. "He's got a job washing up in a caff and won't be back for a bit, so sit down and warm up."

Sandy's legs folded gratefully. A blanket from a pile was draped round her shoulders and the young man squatted in front of her.

"I'm Roof," he said. "Short for Rufus. This is our squat – like it?"

Sandy looked around dubiously. The room was lit by an old-fashioned lantern standing on a wooden crate in the centre of the room. Some warmth was coming from a metal paraffin stove, one of the old round sort. There was a camping gas stove standing on another crate near the empty fireplace. Two sleeping bags were folded up against one wall and a pile of blankets and cloths of some sort lay against another. A blanket was firmly hooked over the window as curtain and insulation against the weather.

Sandy looked at the two mugs on the floor by the lantern

and the dirty plates. The room had a damp musty smell but clearly some attempt had been made to make it cosy – against high odds.

"It . . . it's great," she said. "D'you have anything to eat?"

"I'll get you something. We'll get more when Tone comes in. He brings bits from his work."

He handed her a bag of crisps and a cold sausage. Sandy ate them ravenously.

Roof took the mugs out of the room and she could hear water running. So they had water, then. He returned with a small kettle and lit the camping stove.

"Is there anyone else here?" Sandy plucked up the courage to ask.

"Weeell," Roof drawled with humour, "let's say there would be quite a crowd if we let them."

"You mean, you have to keep them out?"

"Got to man the barricades, man," Roof replied. "One of us stays in all the time and we keep the downstairs boarded."

He turned to see to the kettle and make two mugs of tea.

"The council don't bother us that much – it's the other would-be tenants." He spooned out some sugar.

"What are you doing here, anyway – Sandra, isn't it? Run away to the big city?" Roof handed her a steaming mug.

"Sandy, actually." She was pleased that Tony had talked about her and was beginning to feel safer with Roof.

"Yeah," she answered his question. "I don't want to talk about it much."

"Sure. As I say, Tone's on the early shift tonight. He's due about nine. Can't play you any music, I'm afraid."

For the first time since leaving home, Sandy smiled.

"This is dead serious, Sand." Tony looked at his young sister, half anxious, half annoyed. "I mean, the police are going to come looking for you now, and what about school and that?"

The three of them were sitting on the floor around the metal stove sharing the pies and chips that Tony had brought.

"Mum and . . . him . . . they won't bother for a bit. I had to come, Tony, I just had to."

"OK, OK," Tony said quickly to stave off the threat of any more emotion. Sandy had been bad enough when he came in, crying all over the place. He knew what it was like though, poor kid – but what could they do?

"Let's talk about it tomorrow." Roof yawned and stretched. "We got to sleep now."

"Where shall I sleep?" Sandy hadn't thought about that.

"You can sleep in here if you want," Tony shrugged. "It'd be warm for a bit, but we have to turn off the stove."

Sandy looked doubtful. She didn't like the idea of sleeping in a room with two boys, even if one was her brother.

"You can have the back bedroom, can't she, Tone?" Roof had seen her face and got to his feet. "It's not the Ritz but we can fix it up tomorrow. You'll have to sleep on what we've got for now, but . . ." Roof opened his eyes wide and said in a whisper, "I've got a hot water bottle!"

"Blood has been spilt over that." Tony's anxious face relaxed. He scooped up the whole pile of blankets and cloths and led the way.

They crossed the bare wooden landing to a door at the back of the house. Roof was holding the lantern and its pale light made their shadows lurch and swell as they followed him. It was only a matter of a few steps but Sandy felt they were travellers entering a different world. All of a sudden she was unbearably tired.

The room was indeed small. Being at the back of the house, most of the glass in the only window was intact. There was just one cracked pane.

"We'll fix you up with a curtain tomorrow – and some sort of lighting." Tony was speaking to her as he folded and spread layers of blankets on the floor, but his voice sounded far away. "Use your coat as a pillow."

"It's fine," Sandy heard herself saying, longing for them to go so that she could just roll herself up in the blankets and sleep. She stood looking out of the window while Roof went to fill the bottle. There was a dreary little concrete yard below her, full of rubble, ancient dustbins and the like. Nothing grew in it now and nothing probably ever did.

"'Night then, Sand." Tony was relieved that she wasn't scared of the dark.

Sandy was too tired to answer.

Roof came back with the hot water bottle.

"Sweet dreams," he grinned at her. "Ring for room service any time!"

"'Night," Sandy said dreamily. Holding the warm bottle to her she wrapped herself up on her makeshift bed and was asleep at once.

Four hours later she woke up, swimming up out of a dreamless sleep, and lay wondering where she was and why she felt so cold. The lukewarm bottle she was hugging brought it all back and she struggled to replace the blankets that had slipped off her shoulders.

It was dark as pitch. There was nothing to be seen anywhere around her. She felt marooned and alone.

Was that a sound? She strained her ears. The house was very still and no noises came in from the city outside. But yes, there it was again, a faint sound of scratching. It was coming from the bottom of one of the walls near the floor. Sandy couldn't tell exactly where.

"Rotten mice," she thought and tried to roll over – a bad move, as all the blankets fell off. She pulled them back and tucked her head beneath the top one. But by now sleep was far away and the scratching sounded louder. There was an urgency about it. Then it stopped abruptly in mid-scratch.

Sandy shivered. It wasn't just the cold. She shivered because she felt the old black hole reach up for her once more. She knew Tony and Roof were in the front room and tried to gain comfort from the thought, but it didn't help. They were two and she was one. She wondered if her mother realised that she hadn't come home and if she would care. She doubted it.

A new and altogether sharper sense of loneliness mingled with despair filled her. She gave herself over to the black hole, buried her head further under the blankets and cried bitterly for a long time until she slept.

"There are mice in my room." They were brewing tea and eating bread and jam around the stove. The winter light was struggling to get going outside the filthy windows.

The boys looked at Sandy. Roof thought she looked rough. Her face was very pale and there were dark circles under her eyes.

"I heard scratching – all night."

Tony shrugged. "There's worse things than mice." Girls! he thought.

Mid-winter was a bad time to be in a squat. They woke with their blood sluggish and tempers short. Tony wore his hair scraped back in a ponytail and abandoned shaving. His face looked thin and uncared for. London hadn't given him what he wanted, not by a long shot. By day he signed on at the job centre or hung about with others like him. By night he washed up in a wine bar. Somehow he couldn't land the job that would give him enough to get the place of his own he longed for. This squat was the next best thing. He brought in the food and Roof found everything else.

Sandy felt bleak and unhappy. Tony wouldn't send her away, but she hadn't found the brother she needed, the one to make the black hole go away. If anything, meeting him again seemed to have made it deeper.

She lifted her piece of bread and jam to her mouth. Suddenly her throat constricted and she didn't feel hungry any more. She held out her half-eaten piece of bread to Roof.

"Want it?"

Roof devoured it in two bites. He, on the other hand, shaved every day with a mug of hot water. His baggy black sweater was old and holey and his jeans let in the air in many places, but Sandy was getting used to the way he looked.

Even his dreadlocks, falling around his ears, were beginning to look, well, normal.

Tony pulled on his thin denim jacket. "I'm late tonight, Sand. See you." He left, going swiftly down the stairs and through the front door. Roof followed behind him to bolt it again.

They had decided to let Sandy stay with them until the Christmas break was over. Then they'd see.

Later Roof went out too, putting Sandy on guard. This scared her, but he said there wasn't much chance of an invasion or he wouldn't do it. He left her a pile of magazines to read and said he'd be back for lunch.

Sandy stayed by the stove and leafed through the magazines for a while. She wondered vaguely where Roof went and how he had found all the useful things they had. There was something devil-may-care about him. She thought he probably shoplifted. Perhaps he'd let her go with him. They could be a team. She did so long to be a team with somebody.

"Funny sort of Christmas this is going to be," she mused.

She pulled up some old cushions and lay on the floor in the warmth of the stove, daydreaming about her ideal family. She pictured them around the glittering Christmas tree in a cosy drawing room with a real fire and presents piled high. The mother, pretty and fashionably dressed, was opening her present from Sandy, who waited eagerly for the cry of pleasure and hug that would follow . . .

"Sandeee!" Her name floated up at her from outside the window.

She sat up, shaken.

It was Roof and she had to go down and let him in. He was carrying a large bundle.

"Got you a mouse-trap," he told her.

She felt angry with him for breaking into her dream. Anyway, she hated mouse-traps.

Roof went on. "And there's a lilo – only got a tiny hole, better than nothing – and a duvet. Haven't I done well?"

Sandy couldn't raise a smile. "Lovely," she said.

"Tin of soup for lunch, and bread and cheese. A feast, eh?" He needed to make her smile.

She nearly did. There was a tightness in her throat again, making it difficult to get a breath and impossible to think of eating, no matter how hungry she felt. With it came the wave of black despair that had engulfed her in the night.

"And," Roof was still rummaging in his old canvas bag, "I've got you a candle. You'll have to be very careful. And you can wear this old jumper – we'll see about trousers later."

"Where'd you get all this?" Sandy managed to ask.

Roof looked sly. A wide, sunny smile split his face. "Ah,"

he whispered. "Them as asks no questions, doesn't hear a lie . . ." He said it in a comical way, hoping that Sandy would smile.

She tried. "What about Christmas, Roof?" It was a desperate attempt to break through the darkness closing in on her – anything to bring back normality.

"Trust your Uncle Rufus," he replied. "I'm working on it." He went to fill the kettle in the bathroom.

Sandy gave in and the blackness took her.

After his late shift Tony brought in chicken and chips, still hot. Sandy was ravenous but she didn't try to eat anything. What was the point? She wouldn't be able to. The exhaustion she felt yesterday was returning, so she said she would go to bed.

"No mouse-traps," she said as she watched Roof stick her candle into the neck of a milk bottle. When it was lit she carried it across the landing to the back bedroom. The tiny flame wavered in the draught from under the door as she put it on the floor near her bed. Sandy watched the way it threw her shadow, vast and ballooning, on to the ceiling. She felt disembodied, as if a part of herself was floating free with her shadow and out of her control.

It was much easier climbing under the duvet than fighting

with the blankets. Roof had shown her how to blow up the lilo, saying she should give it a top-up if it went flat in the night. She kept the new thick jumper on. The boys had let her have the hot-water bottle again.

Almost as soon as Sandy blew out the candle the scratching began. It seemed to be coming from the other side of the room from where she was lying. Sometimes it was quick, with the scratches coming fast, but other times the sounds were slow and laboured as if it took enormous effort to make them.

Sandy began to hate them, but she was compelled to listen. Try as she might, she couldn't shut the soft, scraping noises out. They filtered into her as she lay in her makeshift bed and made her whole body breathe to their rhythm. In the end she gave herself over to them completely and they mingled with the gaping cavern of her own unhappiness and this newer, sharper feeling that there was no one in the world to care. The sounds became a part of her in a way she could not possibly define.

It was certainly no mouse.

She didn't know if she slept or not. All she knew was she didn't want to get up to do anything about it. She would let it go on for ever if it had to. She just didn't have the energy.

"What's the matter, Sand? You ill or something? You look dreadful."

Tony watched his sister clasping the mug of hot tea with both hands. Her bread and jam lay untouched on the crate.

Feeling the eyes of both boys on her she put her mug down and reached for it.

"I don't feel very special," she said. She didn't. When Roof had called her she had dragged herself up with an effort. It had taken all her will to leave the bedroom and join them for their simple breakfast around the stove.

"You need to eat," Roof told her. "You didn't have anything yesterday. What's happened to that famous appetite?"

Sandy lifted the bread to her mouth, but she had stopped feeling hungry. As she made herself bite it a sharp pain shot through her stomach and she grunted, dropping the bread. Her breath came in harsh, laboured gasps.

"She's got a chill." Roof was beginning to look worried.

"Yeah . . ." Sandy struggled to say.

I must have a chill or something, she thought. I've never felt like this before. She just wanted to go back to bed, to be curled up with the hot water bottle in the back bedroom. That was all she wanted. She'd be OK there. She was feeling better now, just thinking about it.

The boys agreed when she told them. They fussed around with things to make her comfortable. Sandy was grateful, but she was glad when they left her alone.

Tony's voice came through the thin wall.

"What happens if she's really sick, Roof?"

"She's had a rough time," Roof's deeper voice answered. "She needs a lot of rest." Then they moved away.

The grey light of the December morning struggled through the murky window of the back bedroom. It revealed years of neglect which had given all the paintwork, chipped as it was, a veneer of yellow ochre. Its true colour was impossible to guess, as was the colour of the paper that sagged limply in places as it tried to cling to the walls. Layers of it, Sandy guessed as she studied the room. She wondered what the very first paper had been like.

From her bed she tugged at a loose triangle of wallpaper near her head. To her horror it fell away easily, bringing the dust of ages with it in a cloud. Coughing, she struggled up and moved the lilo, shaking it to get rid of the dust. It was in her hair and eyes as well. When it settled she saw shreds of another paper still sticking to the old cracked plaster. This was an ugly brown with some kind of floral pattern. She touched it with a finger and at once another patch of the outer layers fell forward and the dust rose again.

This time a larger area of the brown paper was revealed.

Sandy was wondering if this had been the room's original paper, when she noticed a drawing on the wall. It looked like an oversized doodle in the shape of a circle spiralling inwards until it got to the centre. Then the line plummeted down towards the floor. It had been done with a kind of thick pencil and some of it was rather faint.

Fascinated by the shape, and realising that the marks had been made when the house was young, years ago, she put out her hand and slowly traced the spiralling line with her finger. She wasn't aware of the moment when the scratching began again in the opposite wall because the spiral was beginning to make her feel giddy – almost hypnotised. Her finger paused in the centre of the circle to begin its descent to the floor and, she decided later, that must have been the point at which she became aware of the noises.

She made her finger follow the plunging line until she had to crouch down where it disappeared into the skirting. As its course took it down the wall, so her spirits followed it. They too got lower and lower until, when the line disappeared, despair gripped her once more and she felt afraid.

The sharp pain shot through her stomach again, making her cry out. Then it stopped as abruptly as it had done before. Sandy was left limp and helpless.

She lay on her bed and struggled to think.

"Shut up!" she cried to the now constant scratching. But her voice came out as a whimper and tears of weakness coursed silently down her cheeks.

In desperation Sandy tried the Christmas daydream, but

she couldn't find it. Only the greyness of appalling neglect filled her inner eye, and in that half state she stayed until Roof returned with a bowl of chicken soup.

"Has she been in there all day?" Tony was back from work with packets of warm fish and chips. He had also brought in a tin of ham and a Christmas pudding.

"She tried a mouthful of soup lunchtime and then said she had a pain again. She didn't get up." Roof began to organise the plates. "We'll try her with this. It smells good."

"She ought to come out, where it's warmer."

"I'll get her." Tony heard Roof open the back bedroom door. Then he returned.

"She's asleep."

"She's got to come. I'll go." Tony suddenly felt very anxious. He stood in the doorway of Sandy's bedroom and stared down at his sister. He had brought the lantern and in its yellow light her face had a waxen, artificial look. Always pale, she seemed paler and the dark circles beneath her eyes were like bruises. She also looked thinner.

He hadn't wanted this, he thought. Trouble over Sandy would really mess things up. She had to get better, be OK.

Bending over his sister, Tony thought, she's too young

for this caper. He put the lantern down and stretched out his arms to carry her into the front room.

She wouldn't budge. It wasn't that he couldn't get his arms round her – he did – but she wouldn't budge. She felt as heavy as lead, lying there.

Then, without changing her expression, Sandy's eyes opened and looked at him. She didn't move a muscle. She just looked at him with a blank, empty stare. It was uncanny and Tony backed away.

"I got some fish and chips," he said lamely. "Want some?"

There was no reply.

Then he saw the huge patch of fallen paper and plaster dust. Sandy's bed was half lying in it.

"Roof!" Tony shouted. Roof came running.

"Give us a hand, we'll carry her."

Roof looked at Sandy's blank open stare and went cold. He touched her. She was still quite warm and he could feel her breath.

"Right. You take her head." He bent over her legs and Tony got in position.

"One, two and up!" Both boys lifted but nothing happened. Sandy could have been made of granite. Still she lay there, staring.

Roof grabbed Tony. "Come on. We need help." He pulled him away and into the front.

"Wait!" Tony was breathing hard. "Think! We can't. Think!"

"She's not right."

"She may be better tomorrow. You know what you said about rest. Maybe that's what she's getting. Let's – let's see how she is tomorrow, eh, Roof? C'mon, eh?"

Oh God! If I lose this squat, what shall I do? Tony thought desperately.

Roof turned away. He knew the problem. He struggled with himself for a moment.

"OK. We'll see in the morning," he said to Tony. "But we'll do something then if we have to. OK?"

Tony nodded miserably.

Sometime after that Sandy stirred. The scratching was louder, calling her. I'm coming, she thought. I'm coming. But it was hard to move. Hard to shift her leaden body.

With great difficulty she left her bed and began to crawl across the floor to the other wall. She stopped often to get her breath, whimpering a little. At last she collapsed against the wall, leaving tracks across the dusty floor.

The scratching was in her head now. Scratch, scratch, scratch. She was very close to it.

Scratch, scratch, scratch . . . She raised a heavy hand and

tried to scratch back. Wallpaper crumbled under her nails. She pulled at it and a long strip came away.

Scratch . . . pull . . . scratch . . . pull . . . scratch . . .

Morning came. When Tony and Roof got no answer from Sandy's room, they entered it cautiously.

They found her covered in plaster dust, on her knees against the wall, feebly pulling at the paper. When she saw the boys she turned to them with a ravaged face.

"Help me . . ." She was obviously too weak to stand, but sagged as she knelt, supported by the wall.

"I'm getting help!" Roof turned.

"No!" Tony grabbed at his jumper. "It – it's Christmas Eve. No one's around. Roof, man, we'll manage. We'll get her OK . . . we'll cope . . ." He was floundering and knew it.

Roof's eyes suddenly blazed. He seized Tony by the shoulders. "If you can't see that your sister needs help, if you're too blind and selfish—"

Tony made a fist, desperation twisting his face.

Roof tightened his grip on his shoulders and pushed him hard. Tony staggered across the room, loosing his hold on Roof's jumper. Then Roof swivelled on his heel and was gone.

"Help me, Tony . . ." Tears of weakness were running down Sandy's cheeks.

Feeling desperate, Tony moved uncertainly towards her. He couldn't understand what was wrong. How had she lost so much weight? Why was she so weak? And what was it she wanted him to do, for heaven's sake?

Sandy's fingers, bleeding now, scrabbled frantically at the paper.

"Please . . . please . . ." She doubled over, clutching her stomach.

He couldn't stand it any more. He grabbed a dangling shred of wallpaper and pulled it. Wodges fell away from the damp and rotten plaster. The dust was awful.

"Here . . ." Sandy begged him. "Here . . ."

He lurched through the dust towards her and went on stripping. The next piece that came away revealed the corner of a built-in cupboard. It had been papered over so completely and so often that it had disappeared without trace for years.

"Yes . . . yes . . . go on . . ." Sandy, clutching her middle, was rocking to and fro.

Tony did as she told him. He stopped thinking and just obeyed. Anything to ease the terrible pain he saw on Sandy's face. It didn't make any sense but on he went.

Soon the entire cupboard was free of ancient paper. Tony

took his pocket knife and dug away at the bunged-up edges of the door until they were clear. But there was no latch or handle to pull it open. He stood, undecided.

Sandy slipped sideways, leaning helplessly against the door. Her terrible scrabbling continued.

"Don't! Don't! I'll get something!" Tony heard himself shout as he ran to the front room. At the bottom of a canvas bag was the hammer he and Roof used to board up the downstairs windows. He seized it and rushed back.

"I'll get the damn thing open!" he shouted frantically. "We'll get it open!"

He hit the cupboard door with the hammer as hard as he could. The old wood splintered but didn't break. He drew the hammer back and hit it again and again.

At the first blow of the hammer on the cupboard door Sandy fell onto the floor unconscious.

"My God!" Roof and an older man stood in the doorway. It was a terrible sight. Tony was going at the cupboard like a madman and Sandy lay white and still among the debris.

At last Tony's hammering made a large hole in the wood. His face was streaked with sweat and tears as he turned to Roof.

"Help me!" he shouted.

Roof didn't argue. Together they put their hands through the jagged opening and tugged strongly. The other man bent quickly over Sandy and gently lifted her hand, looking for the pulse.

With a splintering crack the old cupboard jerked open and carried the boys with it. They stumbled backwards.

For a moment dust obscured everything. Then slowly, with a noise that sounded like a sigh, something huddled at the foot of the cupboard tumbled into the room. The boys stared in frozen horror while a heavy, musty smell filled their nostrils. They watched the skeleton of an arm and hand fall, almost gracefully, to lie in the dust next to Sandy's. Under a tangled mass of hair a skull rolled free of the tattered shreds of cloth and lay still, staring at the ceiling with its empty eyes.

Terror filled Tony, followed by a consuming rage against the dead hand which lay beside his sister's lifeless one. He drew back his foot and aimed a kick at the thing, sending the fragile bones spinning over the floor and raising a heavy pall of dust. Then the horror of what he had done possessed him and he buried his face in his arms and leaned against the wall.

Roof put his hand on his shoulder. He turned to the man kneeling over Sandy's lifeless figure.

"Is she all right, Dad?" he asked as the older man rose, lifting her up in his strong arms. She looked as light as a feather.

"Let's get her out of here," his father said. "Got a clean blanket?"

"But, what about . . .?" Roof hesitated uncertainly, unable to look at the broken shape on the floor.

"It's . . . just a bit late for her now," his father replied gently. They made themselves turn to look at her, a dry, dusty heap of bones, with the shreds of an old petticoat still clinging about her legs.

"We'll call the police from home. Come along."

They went with him gratefully.

As soon as she left the bedroom Sandy began to revive. By the time she was in Roof's house she was sitting round the kitchen table with them all, eating a bowl of cereal hungrily. She was pale and much thinner, but her pain and weakness had evaporated. She was free to be Sandy again.

Roof's father was a doctor, and the family house was not far from Portello Road.

Tony was bewildered. He had thought Roof's situation was like his own.

"We guessed you weren't far away," Roof's mother said, making them a late breakfast. "Things kept disappearing from the garage and the attic. We thought it must be you, so we didn't worry."

Sandy raised her eyebrows at him and he squirmed a bit. To hide his embarrassment, Roof turned on his father.

"You went too far, Dad. You needed teaching a lesson."

"You don't change, do you, Rufus?" His father's voice began to rise.

Roof's mother put a plate of hot toast on the table.

"Later," she said firmly. "That's for later. We want to hear Tony and Sandy's story now."

It was difficult for them at first, sitting in this friendly kitchen and realising the yawning differences between Roof's situation and theirs. It made them tongue-tied. Tony felt it most because, unlike Roof, his future was so uncertain.

Roof, he discovered, was going to university next year. His time in the squat had been an adventure exercise, not for real, like his.

But in the end the genuine friendliness of Roof and his parents drew their story from them. As they gazed around at all the Christmas cards and decorations in the cosy room, reminding themselves that it was Christmas Eve, they were glad to be there and tried not to think how it was in their own home.

After a while they all fell silent, relaxing and warmed by the good food.

"I wonder who she was," Sandy said half to herself. "To

112

be shut in that cupboard and left to starve . . ." she shuddered.

"Hmmmm . . ." Roof's father sighed. "The police may find out from old records. At a quick glance, she looked about your age, Sandy, from her size. There was just as much cruelty a hundred years ago, you know. Poor little thing."

"But odd it happened to Sandy." Roof's mother looked thoughtful. "Those end houses are due for demolition in the spring. Perhaps it was her last chance to let anyone know she was there. They'll certainly give her a proper burial now."

Sandy was silent. It wasn't only that, she thought to herself. I think she was forced to wait until someone came who was as unhappy as she had been. She could reach out to them and make them understand what she went through. What it was like to cry and starve in the dark with no one to hear. To sink down at the bottom of the cupboard and scratch helplessly at the door for the last time. And then to die and be walled up and forgotten.

Pity welled up in her, and pity too for her brother . . . and herself.

"One thing," Roof broke the mood. "We're not having Christmas in Number 61. I guess this place will do." He looked around at them. "Ring home. Tell your mother you're having Christmas with friends in London – why not?"

"Why not?" Tony and Sandy looked at each other. They knew they had decisions to make. Sandy knew she would have to return home to go to school, but it was Christmas and a new year was coming.

HUNTER'S HALL

Garry Kilworth

here had been a moment when the sky darkened and the snow-covered forest became still. A moment when the shadows merged, the light fled, and there was utter silence. One second the distant church bells had been ringing their Christmas message through the icicles on the trees, and the next – stillness. The hunter had never known such a silence. He imagined it was like being buried deep in snow. Not a single thing, over the whole earth, moved or made a sound. It struck fear in his heart: a terror which was like a cold shadow itself.

Then came the terrible pain in his chest, followed by the sound of the shot. He thought it was funny, feeling the bullet hit him first, then hearing the sound of the rifle, but then he remembered that a bullet travelled faster than sound. He had often seen the puff of smoke from a far-off rifle, before the sound of the shot reached his ears.

The pain in his chest was over with quickly. Lying there in the snow, his body numb, he wanted to say to his fellow hunters, "I know it was an accident, so don't blame yourselves." But he could not open his mouth, or move his lips.

Then, miraculously, he felt fine again. He got to his feet, brushed the snow from his hunting jacket, and turned to say to his comrades, "I'm still alive." But he found himself alone. All his companions had gone. Strangely, there were not even any marks in the snow where they had been standing. Nothing. Now he could hear birds and animals again, but the distant Christmas bells were still silent. The trees looked the same, but somehow the whole scene had a curious atmosphere.

He began to call out, "Hey, where have you all gone? Jan? Albert? Peter? Wait for me!" because the fear was back with him again.

There was no answer, so he began to walk.

As he battled through the deep snow, he saw an incredible number of animal tracks on the forest floor. Among others he recognised hare, deer and fox. There were also prints which looked like wolf, but he told himself that wolves had not been in the region for at least a hundred years, so he decided it must be some sort of dog. Then he came across the tracks of a wild boar. He was absolutely certain about the boar, being an expert on such creatures. The hunter became very excited and unslung his rifle from his shoulder. What terrific thing it would be to shoot the last wild boar in the forest! He followed the boar's trail until he reached a clearing.

As he approached the clearing, he remembered his earlier foolishness. To be afraid of shadows! How ridiculous! Yet the memory of that terrible moment came back again and suddenly he wanted nothing more than to step out of the forest and into the full light of day. A dramatic change had come over him and over the woodland. The hunter was the same man, the trees the same trees, yet everything was somehow different.

The broad oaks and beeches, the great hornbeams, the tall, stately ash trees were now seen by the hunter in great detail. He was aware, without close study, of every knot and whorl in their trunks and every twist of their boughs. The very course of their sap was interesting. He found himself admiring their shapes and lines. The firs and pines, laden with heavy snow, had all looked the same before. Now they were like individual people to him, all quite different.

Yet there was something frightening about these sudden

changes and new ways of looking at things. This fear made the hands holding his rifle tremble, just as the icicles on the wych elms were trembling. He had a new insight to nature's secrets, yet with this power had come a strange dread. He wondered if it had anything to do with shooting the badger earlier in the day, but he had always taken such opportunities when they presented themselves. He killed such creatures by instinct. The badger had died because it was a wild animal and the hunter was an excellent shot. It was as simple as that and nothing more.

When he stepped into the clearing and felt the breeze on his face, the hunter felt himself relax. Switching on the safety catch of his rifle, he slung the weapon back onto his shoulder. Then he surveyed his surroundings and found himself pleasantly surprised, if not amazed.

Before him stretched a broad lake, frozen silver in the weak evening sun, with patches of reed tucked away in the shallows. Around the lake was grassland, sparkling with frost where it poked through the thin layer of snow. Enclosing the meadows and the lake was the woodland in which he had been hunting that day, with its oaks and elms, its pines and firs.

It was what he saw on the far side of the lake that astonished him, however, for on that shore stood a magnificent building. A low, rambling, timber lodge covering some four or five acres, it rose out of the snow-covered grassland as though it had grown from the landscape.

The hunter took his binoculars out of their fur pouch and wiped the misted lenses. Then he studied this strange dwelling.

From various points on the thatched roof of the massive lodge sprang tall, twisted, redbrick chimney stacks, smoking lazily into the evening sky. The hunter could scc narrow windows of leaded glass, dozens of them, scattered along the walls of the lodge. Two-thirds from the east end, though it was difficult to make out where the corners were, stood two great arched double doors with decorative hinges of solid brass. Snow-decked ivy curled about the wavering eaves, that dipped and ran with wooden gutters, and dropped down to rain barrels at various unlikely intervals.

The hunter, who was fond of wooden buildings, thought the lodge magnificent. Its presence in this setting took his breath away and he found himself hoping it was some kind of hotel or inn, at which he could spend the night.

"Better than bivouacking in the woods," he muttered to himself, for that was what he would otherwise have to do. "Too cold for that kind of thing at this time of year."

The hunter made his way around the west shore of the lake, not daring to trust the ice to hold his weight. He passed some holes in the ice on the side near to the dwelling, as if someone had been fishing. Finally, he came upon the massive double doors, the entrance to the great lodge. Above the doorway a simple sign in German, burned into a slab of oak, read *Jaegerhalle*.

"Hunter's Hall," he said to himself. "Perhaps it *is* a place to spend the night."

He opened one of the doors and entered.

If the magnificent exterior of the lodge had not astounded him, certainly the scene within would have done. The whole lodge seemed to consist of a single enormous room with stone hearths scattered over the wooden floors. The light from the narrow windows did not reach far into the vast room, but made shafts of dying sunlight around the edge. Even though the log fires and lamps lit the centre, it was difficult for the hunter to see the far side. The atmosphere was thick with the scent of pine planks and wood smoke, human sweat and animal skins, mead, ale and cooking meat.

"Wonderful!" whispered the hunter.

Around the blazing hearths sat crowds of men and a sprinkling of women. All were dressed in hunting gear, but many of the outfits were old-fashioned and some of them appeared to date from hundreds of years ago. There were plain green breechclouts, cracked leather jackets shiny with use, fur mittens and gloves. There were deerstalker hats, rough tweed coats, high calfskin boots. There were waxed-skin waterproofs with many pockets, thick winter shirts, and camouflage overalls such as the hunter himself was wearing.

Those sitting or sprawling around the fires were either talking in low voices, or cleaning and polishing their weapons, or both. And such weapons! Guns, bows, spears and all manner of hunting tools. And the guns were not only modern high-powered rifles or shotguns, but barrel-loading flintlocks, single-shot breechloaders and various other old-fashioned firearms.

At the feet of many of the room's occupants sat gun and hunting dogs of all description, from retrievers to springer spaniels to pointers to Irish setters. Like most hunting hounds, they were as quiet and docile indoors as they were active and sharp outdoors.

In the centre of the great lodge was the largest of the fires, and hanging from a chain over its flames, was the biggest cauldron the hunter had ever seen. It was from this huge black iron pot that the wonderful odour of cooking meat and potatoes was issuing forth and filling the room.

The hunter stood for a long while, taking in the scene, which affected him to his very soul. It was the kind of place a weekend hunter dreams of while he works at his job in the city, or travels on a jet to a meeting with people he has no time for outside business dealings. This was clearly a gathering of huntsmen like himself, in the perfect setting.

Feeling a little humble, the hunter walked across to the nearest fire and spoke to a man sitting there, cleaning a long old-fashioned rifle.

"Excuse me, sir. May I sit by you?"

The man answered him, but in French, which he did not understand at all. The hunter walked away from him, feeling bewildered. However, a second man, on the other side of the hearth, called to him.

"Sit by me. I speak your language. We can talk together about tomorrow's tracking or today's success. We can discuss the Christmas Day feast and the New Year hunt. We can speak about the lore of the forest, the run of the game."

Now this was the kind of conversation in which the hunter loved to participate. Gratefully he crossed the hearth and took the place indicated by the speaker, sitting on a deerskin close to the burning logs.

The man was large, with a pleasant moon-shaped face and skin the colour of weathered mahogany. His black hair was long, hanging over the collar of his leather jacket, and his eyes were deep brown and clear. At the man's feet lay a black Labrador retriever, staring into the flames.

In his hands the man held a breechloading rifle, the barrel of which he was subjecting to a vigorous pulling-through with a cleaning cloth. He offered the hunter a look down the barrel, at the shining spirals of rifling, as the other sat down beside him.

"Good," said the hunter. "Not a spot of rust."

"As it should be," said the man, in a satisfied tone.

The hunter pointed to the retriever, who was now watching him with a movement of the eyes only.

"Fine water dogs, those," he said.

The man patted the dog on the head and received a lick on the hand as acknowledgement.

"Yes, wonderful beasts. This one has been with me for a long time now, haven't you old girl? She doesn't like the winter months though. Not enough for her to do."

The dog nuzzled his hand.

"What is this place?" the hunter asked, gesturing with a sweep of his hand around the lodge. "Who are these people? Is this some sort of Christmas Eve gathering?"

The man raised his eyebrows and looked a little sad.

"Ah, you are new? Then you may be in for a little shock, I think, unless you've guessed already."

"Guessed what?" asked the hunter, who hated puzzles.

"These people, as you call them, were all great huntsmen or huntresses when they were alive – as you must have been yourself, for here you are in *Jaegerhalle*. The place we are in is of course the lodge where we now reside, sleeping around our fires, preparing for the next day's hunt . . ."

The hunter smiled.

"You're making fun of me," he said.

The man stared at him with serious eyes.

"No, I do not joke. You are dead, my friend, and in the hall of the great hunters. No one here can remember what they were called in life. Do you have a name?"

The man then concentrated on cleaning his gun, seemingly allowing the hunter time to think about what he had said.

The hunter tried desperately to recall his own name. How could he forget such a thing. Yet there was nothing there, not even a hint of who he was or what he was called. His mind remained a complete blank on that point. He knew *what* he was, but not *who* he was, nor who his parents were. All he got from a searching of his memory was a feeling of frustration.

Wait a minute! he thought triumphantly. I can feel my own heart beating in my chest! Or was that illusion? Was he breathing, or simply going through the motions of breathing? Surely he was being made fun of, the object of hunters' humour, an initiation ceremony on first entering the lodge. Yet there were no others within earshot to enjoy the joke. Only his dark-haired companion, intent on servicing his rifle.

The man was looking at him again, with quizzical eyes.

"What," said the dark-haired man, "is the last thing you remember before the sky darkened and the stillness came?"

This question shocked the hunter dreadfully. It meant the man knew about the incident in the forest. How could that be, when the man had not been there? Perhaps the man had been hiding behind a tree? Surely he would have come to the hunter's assistance if he had? And in any case, something had happened *inside* the hunter, as well as outside.

"What do I remember?" he repeated, and received a nod from his companion.

What *did* he remember? Why, he and his friends had been tracking a stag, an animal with magnificent antlers. His first shot had struck the beast in the flank, wounding but not crippling. The stag had run, of course, a ragged route through the trees, and the hunters had followed the trail of blood, and then the tracks in the snow when the blood had dried on the wound.

Then what? There was a sort of dark area in his memory after that, between tracking the stag and the moment when the sky closed and silence fell. It was as if his mind was a shade in which a memory was hidden. The memory wouldn't come out. So he had to concentrate, to try to understand its shape, though it attempted to remain vague. As he focused intensely on that dark area, the memory began to emerge, gradually. The reason it had remained hidden was because it was so harrowing that the hunter had subconsciously thrust it away, not wanting to remember something so appalling.

Yet here it came, out of the murk.

Why, yes – he had been standing between two pines when the stag appeared again, to his left. He recalled trying to swing the rifle round, but the strap had caught on something – a branch or a bush – hampering his aim. Then . . . the stag had come on, at speed, its antlers lowered in a charge. Someone else, one of the others, had then aimed and fired.

A sudden flush of fear. Terrible pain. Blood coming out of his chest and mouth in gouts. Then the darkening, the silence. These were his last memories.

Dead? he thought. *Am I dead?*

The thought must have shown in his eyes, for the other man said, "I'm sorry."

"I'm still not convinced," said the hunter. "But I'll go along with it for now."

His new acquaintance shrugged.

The hunter then stared around the lodge at the other hunters. Indeed, they were a strange mixture of men and women, the majority of them with the appearance of being from the past. The Hall of the Hunters? How wonderful if it were!

He spoke to the other man again.

126

"What happens then? To us . . . dead?"

"What happens?" the man smiled broadly. "Why, what happens is, you *hunt*. The lake outside is stocked with every kind of fish: carp, salmon, trout, even minnow. The forest around the lodge has wild boar, deer, hares . . . You see that woman over there?" he pointed to a slim huntress who was waxing the string of her bow. "She can hit a hare on the run, pinning it to the earth with a single arrow. Pheasants, quail, wildfowl of every description – you name it, it's here.

"Yes, the hunting here is good. The best. And everything we kill during the day goes into that pot you see, making the best stew you have ever tasted. Here of an evening, in the great lodge, we feast. We eat, we drink, we enjoy our stories, and the next day – why, it happens all over again! Those creatures we killed the day before rise again out of the woodland mosses, out of the lake mud, out of the bark of trees. I have shot the same boar seven times now, and still he runs the forest tracks.

"Tomorrow, of course, is the greatest banquet of the whole year – the Christmas Day Feast."

If this is death, thought the hunter, it is better than life.

"Is this heaven?" he asked his companion.

"I should say so, though it can be hell too."

Hell? That sounded ugly. But the hunter was not curious enough at that moment to ask about the dark side of death.

127

He was content only to bask in the comradeship of fellow hunters and enjoy what had been his reward. The Hall of the Hunters! How he had dreamed of such a place!

"If that is so," he asked the man, "where are the really *great* hunters of the world? For instance, I see no pygmies here. Where are the Efe of Zaire? Where are those small dark hunters who excite their hunting dogs with cries and songs, to flush out the quarry? Where are those renowned little archers?"

The man shrugged, a gesture which seemed typical of him.

"There are a few hunters from other parts of the world, here in this lodge, but mostly they prefer their own type of hunting grounds, the ones they were used to in life. Those two men over there are Australian Aboriginals, and in the far corner behind the great hearth you will see a group of Iban Indians. There are others. We join together for feasts from time to time, and try each other's hunting grounds.

"There are great hunts in which we all become involved together, and afterwards we exchange stories and talk about our different skills. Here in Hunter's Hall you will see mainly those who have been touched by the mysticism and legends of our own land, by the beliefs of our forefathers. Those who hunted in the bush during life, or in the jungle, or across the snowy tundra, usually want the same landscapes after death. The Inuit do not want to hunt in our forest all the time, neither do we prefer their icy wastes. But there is nothing to stop you doing so, if you wish. You can hunt in any landscape you like, or on the sea. It's your choice."

"I think I understand."

There was silence between them now. All that could be heard was a murmuring around the room as hunters told hunters their tales of the hunt. It was their one source of entertainment for the long, lazy evening hours, when the dying sun shone through the tall windows into the dimness of the great room. The hunter breathed the scent of burning hickory chips and sighed in contentment.

The dark-haired man then engaged his attention once more.

"Tell me," said the man, "the *best* hunt you ever had in your life."

The best hunt? A surge of excitement went through the hunter's breast. Oh yes, the very best of hunts. But could he tell this man about that time, on so short an acquaintance? He decided he could not. Instead, he recounted the time he had tracked and killed the wolves.

" . . . they were the last wolves left in Scandinavia, an old pair but still very dangerous. And tricky. They threw me off the trail several times, I can tell you! I tracked them over the snow and shot them outside a cave. The whole thing took many weeks. It was a great experience."

A frown had appeared on the brow of the other man.

He said, "Did you not eat the flesh? Or did you need the pelts to keep from dying of the cold? Or perhaps the wolves attacked and killed a child . . .?"

The hunter, puzzled by his companion's questions, shook his head vigorously.

"No, none of those. You don't understand. I killed them for sport. For the *thrill* of the hunt."

"Then," said the man, "I cannot understand why you are here, in this lodge. Here we have only huntsmen who killed out of necessity, or to protect themselves or their families. This is the mark of the true hunter, the real hunter, who kills to feed or clothe himself, but not simply to see blood."

For a moment the dark-haired man's words stunned him, but then the hunter shrugged and said, "I am here."

Suddenly he had a great desire to shock this man, to whom he was beginning to take a dislike. He decided to tell his self-righteous companion the story of the greatest of all hunts, the greatest of all prey which he himself had once hunted. If the dark-haired man did not like it, there were others to talk to in the room.

"I once stalked the most cunning creature on this planet," said the hunter. "I pursued him, tracked him down, and killed him where he stood. Never has anything equalled the moment when I squeezed the trigger and saw

130

him jerk backwards to lie in the dust, a bullet from this very rifle in his heart."

The man stroked his dog, not looking at the hunter now, and asked, "What quarry would that be?"

"A man," said the hunter.

Now the brown eyes flickered to his face and he felt satisfaction, knowing he had disturbed the owner of those eyes.

"Yes," he told the other, "a manhunt. One night we captured . . . it doesn't matter who or what he was, except that he was a human being, a man. We let him go into the wood, then we went after him. It was my shot that killed him."

There was a long silence between them, until finally the man stopped stroking his dog and looked up. His eyes were full of sorrow and pity.

"You killed a fellow creature," he said, "one of your own kind – for *sport*. Now I understand why you are here. This will be your only night in the lodge, to give you the opportunity to witness and experience what you *might* have had, what you have thrown away. Tomorrow you go into the forest."

The hunter felt a certain fear at the other man's words, but he added quickly, "As you will go yourself."

"But I go as a hunter," said the man. "You will be the prey."

The newest hunter felt a bolt of terror go through him at these words, and he looked about him, his mind in a turmoil. He glanced at the other hunters cleaning their weapons, at the soft rugs on which they would sleep that night, and finally his eyes rested on the cauldron – the great stew that would be eaten before retiring.

A feeling of faint triumph trickled through his mind, bringing with it hope. Something was wrong with the logic of his fireside companion. There were surely errors in the rules, the laws of this place. Perhaps the dead told lies and the truth was still to be revealed? Maybe the mistake was not yet his? Possibly these things were not set in stone, but could be changed by clever argument? He would not accept what had been said to him without further dispute.

"Ah," he said to his disapproving companion, "but there's something wrong here. You told me a moment ago that what the true hunter kills must be eaten. That means if I am to be the prey, and you kill me, you must eat me. Are you then cannibals?

"Even if I am changed into a beast, to be hunted and killed, over and over again, for all eternity, I am still in my soul a man. I may not keep a man's body, but I will always have his spirit, which can't be altered because it is *me*.

"Do you hunters, you *great* hunters, eat the flesh of your fellow men? Do you gnaw on the bones of your comrades?

Do you drink the blood of your own kind? Are you then going to hunt and kill me, then *eat me*?"

The black-haired man looked deep into his eyes.

"No, of course we won't eat you," he said. "But we have to feed our dogs."

THE CROSSING

Joe Boyle

ean Connery had never been to Fleetwood. Even though his grandparents had lived there all their lives, and his own father had grown up there for the first fifteen years of his life, Sean himself had never set foot in the place.

If I tell you that Sean Michael Connery lived at number fifteen Brownlow Hill, Douglas, Isle of Man, you may realise we're not talking about the film star of that name, not the James Bond of the late sixties and early seventies. True, he had been named after the famous man, because Connery the star had been a hero of his father, David, but there any similarity ended, for our Sean Connery liked nothing better than the simple life, and asked nothing more, in general, than to be left in peace with a good book.

Sean's father was a photographer, and his mother a travel writer, and Sean had done his fair share of travelling in his fifteen years, accompanying his parents on their work trips, usually somewhere in Europe. As he got older, he joined them for weekends and school holidays, and lived with the housekeeper, Anna, whenever his parents were away in term time.

It had been a lonely life, but Sean had grown used to being on his own and was quite capable of amusing himself, in fact, he actually preferred his own company to the company of other people. Which was why, once again, he was not looking forward to Christmas.

His mother and father had been in Windermere for the past two weeks helping to compile a booklet for the Lake-lands Tourist Board, and, since Christmas fell right at the end of their two-week stint, they had decided to stay on for the festivities. Well, as Sean knew, his *dad* would have decided, and as usual his mum would have had to agree. Sylvia Connery never got any choice in these matters, and had learned long ago that her husband always got what he wanted – at any cost.

The instructions Sean had received from his father over the phone had been quite clear: he had to catch the eight o'clock evening sailing from Douglas to Heysham that night, to be met by his parents and taken back to Windermere for the festive period. There had been no point in protesting; the tone of his father's voice, as usual, had left no room for that, and Sean had hung up feeling quite depressed, and made for his bedroom to organise his packing. It was going to be another O.T.T. Christmas.

Sean had always envied the thousands of families who spent the festive season in an orderly, civilised manner, with presents around the tree, church service, turkey dinner, carols and the like.

Christmas in Windermere, though a little isolated, threatened to be like every other Christmas he could remember, no different from Christmas in Munich, or Christmas in Madrid, or Oslo, or Lisbon, all of which had been vulgar, loud, brash, drunken and unbearable.

Last year's Christmas had been in Amsterdam, and his father had brought every inhabitant of every club in the city back to their rented apartment, or so it had seemed. The Christmas Eve party had gone on until midday on Christmas morning, with Sean being shown off like a prize exhibit into the small hours.

It was one thing being someone your father could be proud of, but quite another to feel 'owned'. And his father did treat him like a possession – something to be taken out, dusted off, and held up for everyone to see.

137

"My son," David would proclaim loudly. "This is my son, Sean. Sean Connery."

Then someone was bound to mimic, "The name's Bond – James Bond," and Sean would squirm with embarrassment and feel like hiding from the noise and the din and the humiliation.

That was when he would remember the reason for his father's Christmas excesses. His mum would persuade him to go along with it all, reminding him of what had happened all those years ago, and why David Connery had to surround himself with noise, music and people, at this time of the year.

Sean took a shoebox from under his bed, and from it he extracted an old photograph, one he'd found behind a mirror in the attic a few years ago. It was of a young couple pushing an infant in a pram along a seafront promenade, and in the background was a lighthouse. It was a photograph he treasured – the only one that existed of his grandparents; the infant in the pram was his father, it said so on the back.

Twenty years ago, at Christmastime, a fire had raged through the tiny terraced house in Fleetwood, Lancashire, where David and his parents had lived. The Fire Officer had said that a malfunction of the lights on the Christmas tree had started it, but by the time it had burned itself out, David's parents (Sean's grandparents) had been burned to death. David himself had survived unhurt, but as a fifteen-year-old orphan, had eventually been sent to live with an aunt in Douglas.

He never spoke of the incident, neither would he ever speak of his parents or his childhood. His way of coping with the memory of that awful night was to hide himself behind forced joviality on the anniversary of it every year.

Sean propped the photograph on his desk, and prepared to go off to the shops to purchase presents for his family. Simple items, as usual, but ones he made sure he'd given thought to, in complete contrast to the gifts Sean's father showered on *him* every year. Bags of them, all shop-wrapped, all things he didn't need, and didn't want; piles of items he knew his father had simply pointed to and paid for to be delivered. At the risk of sounding ungrateful, they meant nothing to Sean. He would rather have had one small gift, chosen with love, than all the others put together.

It was almost as though his father was trying to make up for something, but what? All the years of leaving him on his own? Hardly. Sean was a born loner anyway, everybody knew that. There was never a flood of presents on his birthday, only at Christmas. What was his father trying to prove? It was something that Sean had thought about long and hard on more than one occasion.

The plain fact was that David Connery lived for his son,

some would say lived *through* him, and Sean was painfully aware of it. He was aware also, of course, of how much he was cared for – "loved" wasn't a word easily associated with his father, but for all that, the annual shower of gifts was meaningless, and for some years already, Sean had been giving most of the presents away to a Society for Needy Children without his father even noticing that they had gone.

The stores were thronged with people, and there was a Christmas "buzz" in the air which Sean found he couldn't quite tune in to: there wasn't much point, his Christmas was destined to be spent miles away from here, with strangers. He bought the porcelain ballerina figure he knew Anna wanted, and the antique brooch he'd reserved for his mum, and the compilation of Ian Fleming stories he'd ordered for his father was awaiting collection, so, armed with sufficient wrapping paper, he headed back home. There would just be time to wrap them, give Anna hers, have tea, then make for the ferry terminal.

Dusk was falling as he got back to his bedroom, and he switched on the lights of his own miniature tree, and drew the curtains. He glanced often at the photograph on his desk whilst he wrapped his gifts. What kind of people had his grandparents been? What was it about his father that made him want to erase their memory completely? There was something more to it than the fact that they had died in an accident, Sean was certain. What *had* happened that Christmas twenty years ago?

He sat, and took the photograph in his hand, studying the obscure faces, imagining what it might have been like to know them, savouring the stillness and the quiet which he knew could never be a part of any Christmas for him.

The taxi dropped him at the ferry terminal in good time for boarding. The presents he'd bought nestled in his holdall as he crunched his way to the department lounge, his breath forming quick clouds before his face in the cold night air. In the departure area, he found his fellow passengers were few indeed: there were mostly couples of varying ages, one or two families with children, but nobody his age at all.

Not many people left the island at this time of year, but most of those who did flew to mainland cities. He would have flown himself had there been an airport near Windermere. The boats had certainly done better business when they had sailed into Fleetwood, but with this crossing now terminated, the Morecambe Bay port of Heysham was the only stopping-off point out of season.

Sean knew all the boats, and was happy to see that they were to board the *Snaefell*; he knew her to have a good motion, dependable in rough weather – not that the sea tonight was rough at all.

It was a chilly night, and once aboard, most of the passengers lost no time in going below decks to the comfort of the dining area. Sean, however, felt restless, and after padding aimlessly around the inner lounges for a while, he decided to go up on deck where the fresher air might clear his head.

It was a clear, crisp night, with the forward motion of the ship adding a knife edge to the cold. Stars blinked out of a velvet black sky, and the North star in particular gleamed like a distant jewel. What little moon there was cast a pale sweep of light over the surface of the water, picking out the churning wake of the vessel, which Sean could see, as he stood on the stern, trailing out behind and into the distance where it lay like a flat ribbon long after the boat had passed.

The lights of Douglas could still be seen sparkling from afar, and to the left, the beacon at Dreswick Point, with Laxey over on his right hand side. He was the only soul above decks, encapsulated in a moment of complete isolation, his senses hijacked by the dull, rythmical thud, thud, of the engines, the swish of the water, and that roistering smell that all ships have at their working end, a mixture of salt and diesel.

He was totally unprepared for what happened next.

Without warning, all sound cut out as effectively as if someone had closed a door. He could still see the creaming wake, feel the thump and vibration of the engines, but for some unaccountable reason – no sound!

He looked about him wildly, anxiety gnawing at his chest, then, just as suddenly, from his right came a flash – if something that lasted longer than an instant, as this did, could be called a flash. It was as though someone had swung a shiny sword in an arc, from his right over to his left, from horizon to horizon; and with it came a noise such as might be heard in a sawmill, that ringing, zinging whine as a revolving saw slices through wood, a sort of *ssszzzzuuuuddd*!

The whole thing lasted maybe two seconds, before the hearing shot back into his head with such suddenness that he flinched. Once again the beat of the engines and the churn of the water resumed – though not quite as before.

His first instincts told him that the pace had slowed, the wake was less turbulent, the engine noise less thrusting. A less observant person would have settled for that, but Sean had stood and listened to enough engines on enough Irish Sea crossings in his life to realise there was something more to it than that. Unlikely as it might seem, it sounded almost as though he was listening to a different engine. His eyes followed the ship's wake, and what he saw at the end of it brought a puzzled frown to his brow.

The lights of the now distant island, so visible a moment before, had disappeared.

For what seemed to him a long time, but could only have been a couple of minutes, Sean stood, gripping the rail, trying to work out what had happened.

Things felt . . . different. He couldn't explain how, but even the smell was different from that which he remembered before the interruption.

He looked back down the boat. The decks were still deserted, and the funnel, taller than he remembered it, was beginning to reflect the ever-increasing glow in the sky as dawn broke on the port side.

Could he be imagining all this? Perhaps he had the beginnings of a winter chill, a virus of some kind. His head had been muzzy before he came out here.

But, wait a minute . . . the *dawn*? How could that be possible?

They had left port on the eight o'clock evening sailing . . . that couldn't have been more than twenty minutes ago, and yet . . . He felt his scalp prickle with apprehension.

He could see now that beyond the prow of the boat there was land, and fairly near, too. But how could that be? The crossing to Heysham was three and a half hours and . . . a possibility registered . . . he must have had a blackout, yes, that's what must have happened.

144

He looked at his watch, and was startled to see that it showed six-thirty.

A wave of sickness lurched over him that had nothing to do with sailing. He swallowed hard, picked up his holdall, and slowly walked towards midships.

As they neared the shore, people began to emerge from below, obviously preparing to disembark. Sean eyed them warily. Where on earth were they all coming from? There couldn't have been more than fifty passengers on board, yet suddenly, here were crowds! And he didn't remember seeing any of them before. These people were of a different type, dressed . . . differently, and in clothes which seemed strangely dated. There were many more families with children, and up by the bow he could see what looked like a school party of youngsters around his age, larking and pointing excitedly ahead.

Fear knotted Sean's stomach. This must be a nightmare. He must be lying in bed dreaming all this, and any moment he'd wake up. Or else – that was it – he'd made a genuine mistake, boarded the wrong boat. His hope sank as quickly as it had risen; there was only one sailing, one destination, Heysham, and nowhere within twenty minutes sail of the island.

An object floated past on the starboard side. A pier. A pier?

He stared at it. A Victorian pier, with an amusement arcade at the end. There were men fishing off this one.

Heysham didn't have a pier!

Where exactly was he, and who were these people? His eyes fell on a brass plate bolted to the back of the ship's bridge. It bore the name of the ship he was on, and it read, quite distinctly, *Lady of Man*.

He looked around more carefully, and the more he saw, the more he realised that this, indeed, was that ship, an older vessel altogether.

They were now speeding up an estuary, and the town they were sailing into hove into view. There was a small beach, a lifeboat station, a tall inland lighthouse (vaguely familiar) set amongst streets of terraced houses. The promenade bordering the beach was not a hundred yards from the ship's side as they sped by and Sean noticed a hotel – the 'North Euston'. Then the ship was docking, its engines complaining as they were thrown into reverse to slow it to a stop beside a quay.

Men in blue jerseys stood ready to throw the ropes out to others who waited on the quayside to secure them to bollards, and the passengers crowded towards the spot where the gangplank would be set up. Jostling, shuffling, they surged forward, and Sean was caught up in the push to disembark, his heart thudding with alarm, his knees suddenly weak with disbelief.

It was then he saw the name, in red letters on a white background, of the place at which the *Lady of Man* had docked. The blood drained from his face as he read: FLEETWOOD DOCKS AND HARBOUR BOARD.

He began to struggle, fighting not only against the tide of people, but against the idea of what was happening to him. Panic bubbled in his throat as he tried, vainly, to prevent himself being taken from the ship. A few of the passengers looked mildly surprised that he was facing the wrong way, but no one seemed unduly concerned.

"Watch what y'doing lad," said one man, but there was no threat in his voice, and the warning was obviously meant kindly.

He had reached the lowered gangplank now, and once inside its restricted width, and with the downward slope, it was useless to struggle.

Quite suddenly, the throng emptied out onto the quayside, and Sean was bustled and buffeted to the fringes of the crowd. He stood, clutching his bag, panting with the effort, and watched as the people streamed away in their groups, wishing each other "Merry Christmas" and "All the best for the New Year."

The school party went chattering past. Some of the girls looked at Sean and smiled, then giggled to each other as they trooped off, arm in arm. One or two of the boys threw a

147

"See ya!" in his direction, but they'd gone before Sean even realised it was him they were speaking to. He was still standing, motionless, beneath the red and white sign as the last stragglers departed.

Alone, the enormity of the situation began to descend on his shoulders like a big, black vulture. He tried to think logically, sort out the chain of events which had landed him here. The facts were that he was in Fleetwood, but there had been no sailings from the Isle of Man to Fleetwood for the past – Lord knows how many years. He had just got off a boat he hadn't boarded, and then . . . logic deserted him. The one question his mind kept throwing up was, why?

A figure was silhouetted against the sky at the top of the slipway. It was a woman, and he watched as she slowly made her way down to where he stood. There was something he recognised about her, the way she walked perhaps? As she approached, and her features became visible, the familiarity became even more marked, something about her eyes reminded him of someone he knew. He judged her to be about fifty, and she stopped a few metres from him, as though unwilling to approach nearer than that, her hands clasped nervously across a coat that looked too thin for the cold.

"David?" she said, timorously, "Aren't you coming home?"

He stared at her, open-mouthed.

"David?" she repeated.

He licked his dry lips, found his voice.

"I'm Sean," was all he could say.

The woman gave him a thin, brief smile.

"It's warmer at home," she said.

She made no attempt to touch him, just turned, walked a few steps, then waited for him to follow. In a daze, not quite knowing why, he did so.

The slipway led out onto a broad road lined on one side with a terrace of Edwardian houses. There was a public garden fronting the hotel he had seen, and in between the two ran a tram track which skirted the inland lighthouse. A couple of cream and green trams, of a design which could have been called "streamlined" a good few years ago, rattled past.

"Did you enjoy yourself?" the woman asked.

She was obviously under the impression that he was some-one else, and Sean felt it was time to put things straight.

"I don't think I'm the person . . ." he began. Then another tram rattled past and drowned what he had to say.

She walked on across the tram track, looking over her shoulder, and again he felt impelled to follow her. He caught up with her on the other side of the road, anxious now that he should state his case.

"Did you hear what I said?" he almost shouted.

A look of fear stole over her face, and Sean immediately regretted his tone of voice.

"My name's Sean," he said more softly.

"If you like," she said, and again the thin, brief smile, almost in pity. "Your father might have a surprise for you when you get home," she continued, glancing nervously to see that he was following.

"My father?" he muttered, stumbling hesitant after her.

"We've been doing some thinking while you've been away. He said to me, he said, 'Mother, our David ought to have that what he wants.'"

Mother? David? His *father*?

She thought she was his mother! It was then the familiarity he'd seen about her registered with a shock: her eyes! Her eyes were exactly like his father's! The same light blue, the same shape! She thought he was David! His father! Then who was she? Surely not . . .

Panic set in. He had to get away! Where to? The boat! He had come on the boat, and if he went back on it maybe everything would sort itself out. Whatever happened, he couldn't go another step with this woman who thought he was her son.

He ran. He didn't see the tram rounding the corner. His head hit its side full on, and he sank to the ground, blackness closing in.

The bedroom Sean awoke in was tiny and cold. He struggled to the surface from a nightmare that had gone on too long, and found himself lying in bed with a bandage around his head. The curtains were drawn, but so thin that the light came through anyway, and a clock beside him, ticking ridiculously loudly, told him it was close to two.

The door opened.

She placed a hot mug of something by the bedside, and drew back the curtains. In this light, it was even more obvious that they were closely related, but Sean's mind still couldn't accept what all the evidence so far seemed to suggest.

"What's going on?" he asked.

"You bumped your head. They would have kept you in hospital, but with it being Christmas . . ."

That wasn't what he'd wanted to know. He remembered the tram car well enough.

"Drink your drink, David."

He wanted to scream at her: "I'm not David! I'm not your son! David is my father!" But the futility of doing so penetrated even the ache in his head. His real feelings must have shown on his face, because the look of fear came into her eyes again, and she took a step backwards.

There was no doubt she *was* frightened of him. He had seen a similar reaction from his own mother on the occasions that his father lost his temper. It had always disturbed him.

151

He reached over and took the blackcurrant drink.

"I've some last-minute shopping to do," she said, timidly, "but your father will be in by teatime."

Sean nodded, too bewildered to argue. She fussed around a little longer, then left quietly, being careful to close the door with the tiniest of clicks.

Sean stared around, and what he saw increased his bewilderment.

Everything about the room suggested that it had been kept the way it might have been twenty or so years ago, from the floral wallpaper and the candlewick bedspread, to the flimsy, woodgrain-effect chest of drawers.

But it was what he saw on the walls that alarmed him. There were pictures of Sean Connery everywhere: Posters of the early Bond films, action shots, Bond's weapons, his gadgets, his cars, his girlfriends . . . There were also racing cars of the time, sleek enough then, but oddly out of date by today's standards.

There was a magazine cutting of an expensive camera, that Sean recognised as a Hasselblad 500C/M, the best that money could buy, and respected by top photographers even today. His father had the latest model.

Why would anyone want to keep a room twenty years out of date? And how come all the cuttings looked new? Surely they would have yellowed with age?

It was when he saw the poster on the wall above his bed that his stomach sank; it was of Manchester United, his father's favourite team, but this line-up included such players as Charlton, Best and Law, and there in the bottom left-hand corner, was the year of the season – 1972/73.

He sank back on the pillow.

This room hadn't just been kept like this. – It *was* like this. Like the people on the boat, the tram cars, everything – it was real. It *was* 1973, this was his father's room, the woman was his grandmother, and he, somehow, had taken the place of his father!

Then another, terrible, thought struck him: it was also Christmas, and he remembered what had happened in a tiny terraced house in Fleetwood, at Christmas, twenty years ago. He put his hands over his face and moaned despairingly through his fingers.

The stairs led down into the only living room, off which was a tiny kitchen, and as Sean stepped into the room a cat, curled by a meagre fire, awoke and saw him. Fear and alarm showed clearly in its eyes as it shot from the room, growling. The furniture was cheap and shabby but clean, and a piece of cardboard covered a broken pane in the window. Over on the sideboard stood a framed picture of his father as a youth, the sort taken by school photographers.

Sean's despair had been replaced by a desperate inquisitiveness. He reasoned that he'd been brought here for a specific reason. No matter how it had happened, the important thing was that he was here, in this house, at this particular time, and given that it was at the time that his grandparents had perished, it stood to reason, as far as he was concerned, that he was here to witness the tragedy. But why?

The fire, he remembered, had been started by faulty tree lights. The tree, a dry spruce, stood in the corner, and he could see how easily it might catch alight, but though it was bedecked with a variety of baubles, there were no lights on it!

A draught of cold air accompanied the opening of the front door, and a tall girl about eighteen entered, her face unsmiling. Her manner was no more friendly, as he was about to discover.

"Back, are yer?" she jibed. "Pity."

She dug her hands in her pockets and glared at him.

"Saw Aunty Mary down the shops, said you'd been head-butting trams."

Mary. His grandmother's name. If she was this girl's aunt, this was his cousin, or rather, his father's cousin.

"It's just a bruise," he stammered.

"Like I said, pity." She wagged a finger in his face. "I've just come to warn you, David."

"Warn me?"

"Yes, warn you. Your mum and dad have been worried sick about getting you that rotten camera."

"What camera?"

"Don't play innocent wi' me! You know what camera. Your dad's pawned damned near all he's got to buy it, and I still don't think he's got enough!"

He remembered the cutting in the bedroom.

"He's not trying to buy a Hasselblad? They can't afford one of them!"

She towered above him, shouting.

"Bit late now! You were screaming blue murder fer one before you went on't school trip to Isle of Man! That was a week ago, and they still can't afford to repair yon window you smashed in yer temper!"

"I did that?" he murmured.

"Well, *I* didn't! but then again, I'm not as spiteful as you. You really will do anything to get what you want, won't you?"

Sean felt tears pricking his eyes.

The picture his cousin was painting was of his father, and much of what she said had parallels with what he knew of him. At times he did bully and Sean's mother was the main victim; he could be frightening in his temper, and yes, Sean had to admit, his father had an underlying violent nature.

It hurt to think that this was the way he had treated his own parents.

The girl scowled menacingly.

"So I'm warning you, toe rag! If Aunty Mary and Uncle Graham haven't been able to get you that poxy camera, just don't take it out on them, right?"

She stepped to the door, then turned. "You spoil their Christmas and you'll have more than a bruised head, you hear me?"

With that, she yanked open the door and was gone. Sean sank into a worn armchair, incredibly saddened, and in no more than a minute, was asleep.

The clink of plates awoke him. His grandmother was laying the table and sitting at it, facing him, was a man he recognised at once, though they'd never met. He was simply an older version of Sean's own father, though the eyes that looked at him now were kinder, more gentle.

"How are you, son?" he said, "Been in the wars?"

"Fine," said Sean, "thanks."

It must have been the "thanks", for a look of surprise passed between Graham Connery and his wife.

The tea was plain, but tasty, and Sean was touched by the genuine affection the couple showed for him, though he sensed that their manner was hesitant.

For his part, he tried, as much as he could to make them feel that they meant something to him too. They were, after all, the grandparents he'd never known, and he owed them the respect, courtesy, and love that it seemed they'd never got from their son.

Gradually, the tension that had been there at the start of the meal eased, and they relaxed and began to smile. Sean felt he was meeting old friends after a long, long time apart, and as they talked and laughed into the evening, he became aware that these were two people whom he loved, and who loved him.

The thought of what had to take place tormented him, and as the evening wore on, he began to think of ways in which he could prevent it happening.

Around nine o'clock his grandmother laid her hand on his. "You're a different lad, David," she smiled. "Whether it's knock on't head, or what, I don't know but . . . yes . . . a different lad." And the tears brimmed in her eyes.

"Look," said Sean. "About the camera . . ." They looked anxious again. "Did you get one?"

The silence, and their shared glances, told their own story.

"Good," Sean went on. "Because I don't want one."

"But – "

"It's not important."

"Are you sure?"

Sean nodded. "What is important," he said, "is that you both know something."

They were puzzled, wary, intrigued. There was a hint of the old anxiety and tension.

"I want you both to know that I love you."

In the silence that followed, the wind rumbled in the chimney, then, spontaneously, the three stood and hugged each other, tears flowing freely.

"Put kettle on, Mother. I've a bit of a surprise."

Graham Connery disentangled himself, self-consciously wiped a tear, and dived a hand into a brown paper bag by the door. Sean shuddered as his grandfather produced a cheap kit of Christmas tree lights.

His shout made his grandmother jump. "No!"

"Lights . . . for the tree." He was confused by Sean's reaction.

Sean backpedalled. If he made a scene now it could only destroy the love and trust they'd built between them these last three hours. He tried to speak calmly.

"We . . . we don't need them. The tree's nice enough."

"Ah, but this'll make it a real Christmas tree. What do you say, Mother?"

"If David doesn't want them on . . ." she began.

"I don't. I really don't," cut in Sean.

His grandfather hesitated, then a twinkle came to his eye. "Well, for once, David Michael Connery, I'm going to do what I want."

Sean watched helplessly as the lights were threaded around the dry, brittle branches, and ceremoniously plugged into the socket.

Was this how it had been? Was this the start of the torment he would have to witness?

Soon afterwards his grandmother suggested an early night might do them some good, especially in view of the episode with the tram, and . . . Sean found himself an unwilling player in the drama he knew was about to unfold.

In a short time, the tree lights would malfunction, and the house would blaze from top to bottom.

But what if he were to unplug the lights? Did the fire have to take place? What would happen if it didn't?

His father (or him?) would go on living in the house, the move to Douglas would never take place and his father never meet and marry his mother. He, Sean, would never be born!

But could he let two people die horribly in a fire just so that could happen?

"Must unplug them lights."

Sean snapped back to reality as his grandfather spoke.

"Saw it in't paper – danger, them are, if y'leave plug in overnight."

He leaned down and removed the plug, and the lights snuffed out.

"Goodnight, son. Merry Christmas!"

"I'll . . . er . . . I'll stay up a bit . . . read," said Sean. He had to think this through.

"Reading now, is it?" said Grandmother, and shook her head. "Different lad, different lad altogether."

Would she ever know how right she was?

He kissed and hugged them, hope rising that there was a chance, after all, that the fire could be prevented, and watched as they made their way upstairs.

Sean sat and thought, and the more he thought, the more confused he became. If he was witnessing what had actually taken place on the night of the fire, how could the fire have started? He had seen his grandfather unplug the lights.

Sean remembered the look of fear in his grandmother's eyes when they first met and how she had avoided coming too near him. He heard again the accusations of the cousin – of how his father always got his own way, no matter what. The wind whistled in the broken pane, reminding him of how it came to be broken.

Did his father know more about the cause of the tragedy than he'd care to admit? Was that the real reason why, every Christmas since, he'd had to drown out the memory of it in senseless revelry? Were all the presents he gave a way of soothing his conscience?

Sean dismissed the thoughts from his mind. The conclusion was too terrible to contemplate. Instead he set about the task of making sure that, if at all possible, the fire should not take place. He stretched the cable on the lights as far away from the socket as possible, and settled down to watch the tree, all night if need be. At three in the morning, his eyes grew heavy. By a quarter past, he was dropping.

He sat up sharply. Something had woken him, but what? Unbelievably, the tree lights were twinkling, scattering shadows over walls and ceiling, and the plug he had trailed over to the far side of the room was there, firmly in the socket.

Instinctively, Sean tried to move towards it, only to find that the chair he was in held him as tightly as if he'd been sewn into it. Helplessly, he could only watch as, with an incredible slowness, the tree began to topple, yet as it fell, it didn't pick up speed, didn't fall with a crash, it was almost as though it was being lowered to the ground by unseen hands.

The tree twitched and jerked as it would if moved around, until the topmost branch sought, and found, the middle of the embers of the fire in the grate.

161

A flame ran hungrily along the thin trunk, spreading rapidly out to the branches, which spat and crackled as they caught alight.

Sean, powerless to move, could only watch, mesmerised, as the tree righted itself, shedding baubles as it did so, leaving an arc of smoke as it swung back into position. It was then that Sean saw the figure of a boy crouched at the foot of the burning tree. Only when he caught sight of the boy's face could he allow himself to believe the unacceptable. Numbly, he watched the image of his own father straighten up and cross to the front door.

The flames flared, fed by a blast of cold air as, behind him, the front door opened, then closed.

On the same instant, the paralysis which had held Sean to his seat, evaporated, and he leapt to his feet.

The tree was now blazing, already the flames were spreading along the floor.

Dense smoke billowed from the foam-backed carpet, choking him, preventing him from shouting a warning up the stairs.

Then paint on the woodwork reached flashpoint and erupted into flame; he had difficulty in seeing, his eyes smarting from the acrid fumes, and suddenly a wall of flame sprang up between him and the stairs.

The fire brigade! He had to get them! It was his

grandparents' only hope. He turned and dashed into the street, screaming for help at the top of his voice.

People came running, ladders were called for, and not one, but a dozen neighbours phoned the fire brigade. There were shouts, screams and thudding feet as the windows burst outwards with the heat.

Sean witnessed it all in a haze of horror. Then it was as though everyone and everything around him, all sound and motion, faded into the background. He could see the commotion on the periphery of his vision, hear the shouts and screams at the edges of his hearing, but as he looked into the flames, he saw not a burning house, but a promenade with a lighthouse in the background, and walking towards him were a young couple pushing a pram. The pram was empty. They stopped, framed in the burning doorway which, to Sean's eyes, wasn't burning at all, and they beckoned to him, smiling.

Sean felt a sudden, irresistible urge to be with them.

Sylvia and David Connery had waited at the ferryport in Heysham long after the last of the few passengers on the *Snaefell* had disembarked. A check with the ferrymaster confirmed that Sean's name was not on the passenger list, and David had begun to get angry.

"He's missed the boat! The young tyke!"

They had tried, several times to phone the house, only to find that the line was unobtainable. It was while they were waiting in the cafeteria, debating what to do next, that the policeman came with the message. The housekeeper, Anna, had alerted them, and the officer had some bad news. Sean had died following a fire in his bedroom. Apparently, the lights on his Christmas tree had malfunctioned.

THE DARK SHAFT

Malcolm Rose

rom his bedroom window, Paul surveyed his new territory. The sky was moonlit, magical and immense. The distant outline of the moor formed a solid, dark wave against the night glow. Nearer, Paul could just distinguish a wide patchwork of fields. Disused crows' nests were black blobs in the stark trees that dotted the moor. Beyond the outhouse at the bottom of the garden, there were several standing stones of ancient granite. To the left, he could see the silhouette of a chimney stack that had once been a vent for the old copper mine.

His eye was caught by a shimmering movement on their own lawn. It was as if a momentary breeze had rippled a small patch of grass and then moved on. Frowning, Paul scanned the garden but nothing else was stirring. He shuddered uneasily. His family had only come to live in Devon three days before so his new home still seemed strange, yet he felt sure that the tremor could not have been natural. Even the merry chirping of a blackbird could not suppress his feeling that there was something odd out there. The place gave him the creeps.

Paul lay down on his familiar bed in an unfamiliar room. Their old home had been on an estate, and outside a street lamp always cast a warm pattern of light and shadow onto his bedroom walls. Now, the darkness of his new room made him feel uncomfortable. He got up, stumbled to the landing and turned on the light, then padded back, leaving his door open. He curled up and soon fell asleep.

At 2 a.m. his eyes opened. At first he didn't know why he had woken up, but then he heard the noise that had disturbed him. It was the unmistakable groaning of the back door. Someone was entering or leaving the house.

Alert, Paul lay still and listened. For a moment, he thought that the person must have gone out but then he caught the sound of footsteps downstairs. "It must be Dad," he said to himself. "I'll go and see what he's up to."

It was a cold night. Paul wrapped himself in his dressing-gown before going down the stairs. Since their arrival the hall had been lined with tea chests and boxes but, after days of endless unpacking, only one chest remained. Most of the downstairs doors were ajar but no light emerged from them. Curious, Paul thought, if Dad was doing a bit of night shift work.

"Dad!" Paul called, not loudly but not too quietly.

Immediately there was a clatter from the kitchen. A man muttered something inaudible, then dashed out. Paul could not see him clearly at the other end of the hall but guessed that he was about the same age as his father. The sturdy figure was dressed in dark and dishevelled clothes and wore an old-fashioned cap. Paul could have sworn that the man turned and sneered at him before he flew out of the back door.

Paul was halfway back up the stairs, intending to wake his parents to tell them what he'd seen, when he hesitated. What had the intruder been doing? Remembering the noise from the kitchen, he went back down, negotiated the last obstacle in the passageway and turned on the kitchen light. A few jars and bottles and the tomato sauce were out on the work-top. The cap of the ketchup bottle had been unscrewed and some sauce had spilled out. It looked like partially congealed blood. The man must have knocked it over when Paul called out. Perhaps he was a tramp looking for food, Paul decided. That would explain the filthy clothes.

He thought twice about bringing his parents down. His dad would probably blame him for the spilled sauce. "You're the only one who touches that stuff," he would say accusingly. Instead, Paul cleared up the mess himself and then went to the back door to lock it.

The key was in the door and it was already locked. Now Paul knew he couldn't tell his mum and dad. They'd never believe him when they saw the locked door. But there *had* been an unkempt stranger in the kitchen and he *had* left that way.

In the morning, Paul helped his dad to put up shelves which his mum quickly filled. Towards lunchtime, she collapsed onto the only part of the sofa that was not cluttered with belongings.

"Well," she said, "I don't know about you two but I don't feel like cooking." No volunteers stepped forward so she added, "Why don't you nip into the village, Paul, and get us something?"

"Oh, all right," he agreed. He made it sound like a chore but really he was pleased to have an excuse to escape for a while and reconnoitre the surroundings. "What do I get?"

"Pasties," his mum suggested.

"Pasties? We're not in Cornwall, you know. Not quite."

His dad interrupted. "They have them round here as well," he said. "When you bring them back, I'll tell you all about them."

"Fascinating!" Paul cried. "Can't wait!"

"We'll crack on," his dad said. "Three days to go till Christmas. I want to put my feet up and have it feel like home by then."

The village consisted of a pub, a church, the general stores and a few stone cottages about half a mile away, a ten-minute walk down a narrow lane. On each bend, the lane swelled into a passing place but there was no need. There were no cars. There was nothing else either. No houses, no play areas, no life. Just hedges and fields.

The lady in the shop was too nosey to serve him in silence. "You just moved into the place up Moor Lane?"

"That's right," answered Paul.

"It be nice up there."

Politely, Paul replied, "Yes."

The shopkeeper smiled. "At your age you aren't into peace and quiet, I suppose. Pity there aren't boys your age round these parts. Still, you'll be at school in Plymouth, I dare say, other side of Christmas. There's plenty of lads for you there."

Paul took the paper bag containing the pasties. "Thank you," he said.

Some way up the twisting lane, Paul saw a boy, perhaps three years younger than himself, sitting on a gate that led into a field where cattle grazed. The boy was staring at Paul inquisitively. Paul was wondering whether he should acknowledge him with a smile or ignore him when the boy called, "You be new around here, eh?"

Paul slowed his pace and replied, "Yes. In the house at the top."

"Your name Pengelly?"

Paul stopped. "Yes. Paul Pengelly. How did you know?"

"Heard Pengellys come back to live here."

"What's your name?"

"Thomas."

He was short and looked sad. His clothes were old and scruffy. His skin was tanned and more weather-beaten than it should have been for a boy of about ten years of age. Paul even spotted open sores on the back of the boy's dirty hands. Suddenly, he felt sorry for the lad.

"Do you live near here?" Paul asked.

"We don't have a home," replied Thomas.

That explains the sadness, Paul thought. Times must be tough here in Devon as well as in the city he'd left behind. It bothered Paul that some people were losing their homes while his own folks hadn't even had to tighten their belts.

"What about school?" Paul enquired. "Do you go to one here or in Plymouth?"

"School? Me?"

"Yes."

"You don't half ask strange things," Thomas answered. "I don't go to no school."

"Everyone goes to school."

Thomas looked wounded. He jumped off the gate into the field. Leaning on the top bar, he cried, "Well, I don't." Then he turned away.

"I'm sorry," Paul said. "I didn't mean to upset you." He shouted after the boy, "Why don't you drop by sometime? Later on today if you like."

Surprised, Thomas glanced back at Paul and called, "I might."

At lunchtime, Paul's dad carried out his threat to tell all about the pasty. As he watched his son smothering the golden brown crust with tomato ketchup, he commented, "Do you want some pasty with your sauce?"

His mum joined in the protest. "Yes. The real thing,

171

these. Not even shrink-wrapped. They'll have plenty of flavour themselves."

"And," his dad added, laying it on as thickly as Paul's sauce, "you can't eat it properly now."

"How do you mean?"

"Fingers," his dad replied. "See this edge of crust sticking out? The men – and boys – down the copper mine used it to hold the pasty in their fingers." He demonstrated on his own pasty. "They'd eat the filling and the rest of the crust but throw away the bit they'd been holding."

"Why?"

"Because the miners got poison on their fingers. There's always a bit of arsenic in copper ore. If they ate what they'd held, they'd have been poisoned by arsenic."

"Why did they take food down at all, if it was that dangerous?" Paul questioned.

"They climbed down ladders to get to the seams in those days. It would take hours, and they didn't get paid for climbing – only for working at the seams. So once they got down, they'd stay for a few days, to make the wages worthwhile. Being down for that long, they'd take several pasties."

Cutting up his own pasty with his knife and fork, Paul asked, "You said boys went down the mine. It wasn't just men, then?"

172

"No. Boys would help out, packing gunpowder and carrying away the ore. Dangerous work in awful conditions, for next to no pay. If you'd been around in the early eighteen hundreds, at your age you'd have been going down the mine for at least four years." His dad paused, and then added, "Except that you wouldn't have. It was your . . . let's see . . . great great great great grandfather who owned the mine. The owner's son would've been spared the copper mine. A Pengelly would have been sent away for schooling."

Thoughtfully, Paul popped the last piece of sauce-drenched pasty into his mouth, chewed, and swallowed. "I suppose my great great great great grandfather would've eaten beef or something while the miners suffered."

"Way of the world, Paul," his dad responded. "Some had the talent to be managers and lived well. Others were only fit for manual work. Just like today."

"But," Paul objected, "docs there have to be such a gap between the rich and the poor?"

"That's just the system. Don't knock it. It's not been bad to us."

"Yeah," Paul mumbled. He felt unexpectedly down-hearted and guilty.

*   *   *

Later in the evening, Paul felt a little queasy. He thought that fresh air might do him some good so he slipped into the back garden for a while. Knowing how dark it would be, he took a torch.

It was a calm night. Paul ambled across the lawn. Involuntarily, he stopped at the place where he had seen the grass shimmer that morning. He put out his foot but something made him hesitate. He could not plant it on that patch of ground. He stepped back a pace. He shone the torch on the grass in front of him and peered at it but could see nothing out of the ordinary. Frowning, he muttered to himself, "Don't be daft!" He forced himself forward and deliberately trod right on the spot. For a moment it felt unsteady, like stepping onto a downward escalator, but this was solid ground. It was going nowhere. Even so, the feeling did nothing to help his upset stomach.

Paul shook his head and carried on walking towards the end of the garden. As he flashed the torchlight about, he thought he caught a glimpse of a face on the other side of the fence. He played the beam near the spot but saw nothing. He shrugged and mumbled, "This place must be getting to me. The kitchen last night, that bit of lawn, and now . . ."

Suddenly, the head reappeared above the fence. Paul jumped nervously and dropped the torch, his heart immediately beating twice as fast.

"Don't be frightened," the face said. "It's me. Thomas."

"Thomas!" Paul exclaimed. "You nearly scared me to death."

"Didn't mean to. You scared *me*."

"Did I?" Paul queried, approaching him. "How?"

"With the light you had in your hand."

"Oh. Sorry. Did it dazzle you?"

"Yes. What was it?" asked Thomas. "How does it work?"

"It's . . . er . . ." Paul didn't know what to say. He'd guessed that Thomas was no genius, but he couldn't be *that* ignorant. "Let me get it," Paul said. "Then I'll show you." He strained his eyes but could not see the torch on the ground. "It must have gone out when I dropped it."

"It be there," Thomas said, pointing behind Paul.

Paul bent down and picked it up. "You must have good night vision," he commented.

He went up to the fence and showed Thomas the torch. "You just slide the knob to here and it comes on. That's all there is to it."

Thomas's eyes glowed with envy. "That's grand."

"Want to try it yourself?"

"Can I?"

"Sure." Paul gave it to him. As he did so, he touched Thomas's hand and felt that the skin of his palm was unnaturally hard, like a dog's paw.

Thomas handled the torch as if it were a precious ornament. He turned it on and shone it across the field. Incredulously, he whispered, "Really grand. Like a miracle, that be. If only I'd had this . . ." He did not finish the sentence.

Seeing the wonder on Thomas's face, Paul did not have the heart to ask to have the torch back. "Do you want it?" he asked.

"Me?"

"Yes."

"Can I? No one's given me nothing before."

Paul smiled at him. "It's yours. An early Christmas present. I can always buy another one." Then he stopped talking, realising that Thomas was staring in awe – or panic – at something behind him. Paul turned round to see his father striding across the lawn.

"How are you feeling, Paul?" he called. "Who's that you're speaking to?"

"Thomas," Paul replied. "He's . . ." But when he looked back over the fence, the boy had gone. He was scampering like a hare across the field, between the rows of standing stones.

His dad came up beside him and enquired, "Thomas?"

"One of the locals. He just shot off. See?"

"Yes," his dad answered. "But if you want a friend, I'm

sure you can do better than that. There must be lads from nice families round here. I don't think this Thomas is your type."

"How do you know? You didn't even speak to him," Paul exclaimed.

"I didn't need to. He looked like a right scruff."

"He's okay. A bit weird, maybe. But okay."

"Well, I think you should look for other friends before you have to scrape the bottom of the barrel." He put his hand on his son's shoulder and said, "Come on. Let's go in. Feeling a bit better now?"

"Perhaps," Paul replied. "But not much."

In the middle of the lawn, Paul came to an abrupt halt.

His father stopped too. Looking puzzled, he said, "What's up?"

"I don't know," Paul said. "It's silly, but that patch . . ." He pointed to the grass in front of him.

"What about it?"

"It's moving!" Paul looked at his father and cried, "Dad, it really *is* moving!"

There was a deep rumbling noise. The grass began to fall away, sucked helplessly into the earth. Where there had been lawn, there was now a gaping hole like a wound. Paul was fixed to the spot, fascinated and frightened. The black mouth opened wider, within inches of Paul's feet, threatening to swallow him whole.

"Paul!" His dad leapt over the hole and pushed him away, knocking him off his feet.

Paul found himself heaving on the cold, wet grass. He moaned, lifted his head, and vomited painfully.

When he'd finished being sick, his father lifted him to his feet. "Let's get you inside," he said anxiously. "And mind the hole."

Paul let his dad steer him round the chasm in the lawn but he couldn't take his eyes off it. There was something malevolent about the hole, he was certain.

Indoors, Paul's mum and dad fussed over him. "You look so white," his mother lamented, stroking his cheek. "And you're trembling."

"I'll be okay in a minute," Paul muttered. "Been sick, that's all."

"And had a scare," added his dad. He went on to explain about the hole that had nearly engulfed Paul.

"What caused it?" his mum enquired.

"Subsidence, I guess," Paul's father answered. "This area is riddled with old mine shafts. You know, down to the copper mine. I think one might have opened up for some reason. I'll get a surveyor in the morning." He turned to his son and asked, "Are you all right now? There's a bit more colour in your face."

Paul nodded weakly.

"Okay," his dad continued. "I'm going out to cover up the hole. I've got some good sized sheets of timber out in the workshop."

"Be careful," Paul's mother warned him. "I don't want another casualty."

Paul sighed. He felt his strength returning and even managed a smile to reassure his mum. "I don't feel so bad. Just eaten something that didn't agree with me, I guess. Must have been that pasty."

"Mmm." His mother looked at him with concern. "You're probably upset with the move as well. An early night and a good sleep's probably the best thing for you."

Paul must have felt poorly, because for once he agreed with his mum's suggestion.

After four hours of deep sleep, Paul woke. His throat was dry and ached for a drink. Even so, he did not relish leaving his warm, safe bed. He lay still for a long time but sleep remained elusive. Eventually, at two in the morning, his thirst dragged him out of bed and along to the bathroom, where he gulped cold water eagerly from cupped hands.

He meant to go straight back to bed but something drew him to his bedroom window. There was just enough moonlight to see the heavy board that his dad had positioned over the hole. He couldn't make out any detail because his vision seemed to be blurred, but he also thought that he saw the door of the outside workshop swing open and shut. He rubbed his sore eyes and then looked again. There was no further movement. Perhaps Dad forgot to lock it after covering up the hole, Paul pondered. He wanted to return to bed yet something drove him to grab his dressing gown, put on slippers and go out to look.

He stood on the back step, shivering and cursing the impulse to investigate. He scratched at the itching skin on the backs of his hands, then set off across the lawn.

He came to a halt when he was a few paces short of the wooden board. He meant to skirt round it but a voice stopped him in his tracks.

"Paul!"

The urgent whisper came from somewhere near the workshop. Paul squinted ahead and caught sight of the outline of the untidy man who had been in the kitchen. "It's Thomas," the man called. "He's sick."

Paul stared in silence, confused.

"He needs you!"

"Me?"

"He be asking for you. Sick, he is. Thinks you can help. Hurry. Over here!"

Paul shrugged and walked directly towards the man. He

stopped again when he realised that he was standing on the board, directly over the hole. He froze, suddenly petrified. The man by the workshop had gone.

Beneath Paul's feet, the board began to shift.

"Oh, no!" Paul moaned. "Please!"

The wood was shaking, threatening to tip him over. Then it began to slide, revealing the abyss underneath. He crouched down to try to keep his balance on the piece of wood as it pitched violently. His eyes were drawn to the dark shaft as more and more of it became visible. He was so mesmerised by the yawning hole that he forgot to concentrate on keeping his balance. Finally the board jolted aside and Paul was pitched over.

From somewhere distant, he heard the reverberation of a yell, "Pa! No!"

He grabbed at the earth and held tight as if he were clutching at life itself. His legs dangled over the hole and kicked helplessly in the air. His trunk lay on solid ground. After the initial shock, he calmed down. Instead of lashing out wildly, he began to inch forward, yanking on tufts in the lawn. Then, with only his feet left hanging over the cavity, he rolled onto his back where he felt more stable. He brought his knees up to his chest and then turned onto one side, away from the chasm.

For a moment he lay on the grass, getting his breath back,

but he did not feel safe. He imagined that, behind him, the dark shaft was somehow still plotting to encapsulate him. He got to his feet and, not daring to look back at the hole in case it bewitched him again, made a dash for the house. He rushed upstairs as quickly as he could and burst into his parents' bedroom.

The doctor arrived before dawn. He gave Paul a thorough examination, prodding here and there, looking carefully at his hands and eyes, asking questions and taking samples. When he'd finished, he turned away and snapped shut his case loudly and deliberately. He watched as Paul nearly jumped out of his skin.

"Interesting," he murmured to himself.

Downstairs, he talked to Paul's mother. "Is he a nervous boy at all?" he enquired.

"Paul? No. Why?"

"He seems a bit on edge now."

"What's the problem, do you think?"

"I'm . . . keeping an open mind at this stage. I need to have some tests done. I've taken blood, skin and hair samples from him, so we'll find out. But at this stage my best shot is some form of food poisoning." He plonked himself onto a seat at the kitchen table and pulled a biro from his pocket. "I need a list of everything he's eaten over the last few days – as much as you can remember. Given that you and your husband aren't showing any symptoms, I'm particularly interested in things he's eaten but you two haven't."

Paul's mum sighed. "Okay," she said. "I'll do my best."

When she had finished dictating the list, the doctor stood up and said, "Good. Let's hope the culprit's there somewhere. All I need now is samples of any left-overs that you've got. Analysis might show up something."

He put the list and food samples in his case, saying, "I'll be in touch as soon as the results come through. In the meantime, keep him warm, plenty of rest, and call me if there are any developments. You can always give him something to settle his stomach and paracetamol to ease any pain. As to the results . . . It's not a good time of year for getting lots of analysis done, with the holiday coming up. I'll push them through as quickly as I can. Possibly the day after Boxing Day."

Later in the morning, Paul's dad called the surveyors. None could come and inspect the hole until after Christmas but they all agreed that it was probably a result of old mine workings below. One suggested that he should erect a fence around it to prevent accidents. After Paul's experience in the night, his father took up the suggestion willingly.

While his dad was outside working round the hole, madly hammering posts into the hard ground, Paul felt well enough to get up. He also felt hungry enough to tuck into a sausage sandwich with lashings of tomato sauce. He washed it down with three glasses of water.

"Come into the lounge," his mum suggested. "There's a surprise for you."

In the corner by the window stood a Christmas tree decorated with coloured lights. Paul smiled limply. "Nice."

"Makes the place look a bit festive."

"Yes, Christmas," Paul mumbled. He was not looking forward to it with the same relish as he had in the past. He lacked enthusiasm because he felt ill and because it would remind him that he was one of the lucky ones while outside the have-nots would simply suffer.

That night, Paul did not have the energy to wander about. He lay awake, scratching incessantly at his hands and feeling the soles of his feet where his skin had become unusually thick. He thought about Thomas and the intruder. The two of them had more in common than their scruffiness. There was a definite resemblance. He wondered if the man was

Thomas's father. He listened to the wind – the first since they'd arrived in Devon. It made the trees creak and the house groan and it even silenced the blackbird. As the night wore on, the wind grew stronger and stronger. By morning, it was a gale.

Christmas Eve. But Paul wasn't in the mood for it. Most of the time he stayed in bed, rising only to get a drink or to be sick. The day passed in a blur. His mum and dad came and went several times to check his health. "How are you feeling?" his mum would ask and, in reply, Paul would mutter encouragingly or just smile. Once, she peered at him closely and said, "You look a bit blue to me."

Behind her, his dad commented, "I think so too. That's more like blood poisoning than food poisoning."

"He's got sores on his hands as well."

After telephoning the doctor, his mum reported back, "The doctor didn't seem that surprised. A blue complexion and skin ulcers are all part of the same problem, he thinks. He's going to put your tests on priority, though. Should be done today or tomorrow."

"Even on Christmas Day?" Paul queried.

"You must be important. Some poor worker will have to be on duty tomorrow just for you."

"I'm honoured," Paul replied, trying to inject good cheer into his voice.

All day, while he drifted in and out of sleep, the wind raged like an invisible madman bent on destruction. Late in the afternoon, Paul felt more alert. He managed to sit up in bed and eat a small meal of baked fish and salad with less tomato sauce than normal.

Eventually his parents stopped fussing over him and went to bed, hoping that their son's Christmas Day would not be spoiled by illness.

When he woke, his bedside clock told him that it was nearly midnight. Outside, the wind pounded on the window like a furious, howling animal. A small draught was getting through the frame and made the curtain ripple uncannily. It was only a wind, Paul knew, but he was afraid that the glass might give way under its fearsome pummelling and shatter inwards. He could imagine the shards of glass ripping through the curtain and hurtling across the room, piercing anything in their path.

He jumped out of bed, convinced that he must escape from the room before the rattling window succumbed to the pressure. He dressed hurriedly and went downstairs. The lounge was lit by the fairy lights on the Christmas tree. Paul stood beside the tree and watched the wind wreaking havoc in the garden. An ugly grey mass of cloud was speeding across the sky, eager to dump its load somewhere else. Below, Paul's dad had cordoned off the cavity by running a rope from post to post. The contraption was resisting the wind's battering. The board that he'd laid on the ground, though, was not so resilient. The wind was getting underneath it and lifting it a little before allowing it to fall back into place. Each time it happened there was a resounding thump, amplified by the hollow shaft beneath.

As Paul watched, a particularly strong gust picked up the board and slammed it onto the ropes. The force of the wind against the upright board made it bow like a canvas sail. The gale vented so much anger on it that something had to give. The whole of the makeshift fence was wrenched from the ground and blown across the garden.

As soon as the wind had completed its task, it died away as if exhausted. The night became still, vacuous, and strangely attractive to Paul. He headed directly for the back door.

From the patio, he could see that something was poking out of the hole. Fascinated, he walked slowly towards it. When he got to the edge of the shaft, he discovered a ladder protruding from it. The rungs seemed to compel him to descend into the blackness. There was no point in fighting the impulse. He knew that the evil in the hole would never leave him alone. He had to face the hostile spirit that had already tried twice to seize him. He just wished that he didn't feel so sick.

He grasped the top of the ladder firmly with the thick skin of his palms. Then he twisted himself so that he could position his feet securely on the rungs, ready to go down backwards.

He had only descended one step, and his head was still above the ground, when he saw the man rushing towards him. It was the slovenly intruder and he was charging straight at Paul with a roar of hatred. Clearly, he was not going to stop. He was intent on crashing into the top of the ladder to dislodge Paul. Just before the impact, Paul loosened his grip and screamed. He plunged into the nothingness and passed out.

Even before his eyes opened, he knew where he was. He was lying, wet through to the skin, on hard damp rock. He could hear water dripping, trickling and splashing. The air was cold and stale. He had fallen inside the old mine. Only the smell of burning oil seemed out of place.

He groaned. His whole body was tender. The pounding inside his head was almost intolerable. He was surprised, though, that he'd survived the fall at all. Things could have been worse.

Reluctantly, he opened his eyes. He had expected nothing – just blackness – but the tunnel in which he found himself was dimly lit. He rolled over and caught his breath. Standing above him was the ghoulish man who had run at him with such overwhelming spite, causing his fall. He was holding an oil lamp at shoulder height.

In a tone that betrayed intense malice, he said, "At last I have you where I want you. In the belly of the earth."

Paul sat up, wincing at his various pains. "Who are you?" he asked. "Why do you hate me so much"?

"Hugh be my name. Pengelly be yours. That's why I hate you," he snarled. "You being the master's son."

"What?"

"You Pengellys have your fancy houses and fancy food, while down here us miners do your dirty work for a pittance."

"But that was ages ago," Paul protested. "We've got nothing to do with the mine now. It's not used any more."

Hugh stared at his young victim and hissed, "You still be the master's flesh and blood."

"Look . . ." Paul did not continue. He thought better of arguing with a man who was likely to flare up at the slightest provocation. He moved his aching legs into a more comfortable position and asked, "Are you Thomas's father?"

"That I be." The venom in Hugh's face turned to compassion as he sighed and added, "Thomas who died down here at two o'clock on Christmas morning."

"Died?" Paul enquired, softening his tone. "How?"

"Thanks to your father," Hugh growled, "we barely had the price of food. When my Thomas did his shifts down here, he had to grovel for crusts. Only way he could stay alive. He ate them despite the poison, he was so hungry." Hugh pointed at Paul. "If you Pengellys had paid a living wage, we could have bought enough food."

Sympathetically, Paul asked, "Thomas died of arsenic poisoning?"

"No. The poison made him weak. He left here at midnight, Christmas Eve, it was. He went up hoping he'd get a Christmas box. We couldn't afford no present, though. At least it'd be a day off work. A day without poison. But he was so weak," Hugh complained. "Two hours on the ladders was too much for him. By the time he smelled fresh air, he was finished. He slipped from the ladder and fell down the shaft . . ." His voice, once loud and vindictive, now smouldered with sorrow. "Where's the justice in that? He was just a young lad, nine years old."

The damp walls of the cavern glistened by the light of Hugh's lantern. The wretched tears that rolled down his dirty face also shone.

"I'm sorry," Paul said quietly. "I really am."

Emerging from his nightmare, Hugh raged, "Sorry is not enough!"

"What do you want of me?" Paul queried, fearing that he already knew the answer.

"Justice."

"What do you mean?"

"Show me your hands," Hugh ordered. He bent down and brought the safety lamp near one of Paul's hands. He saw with satisfaction the thick skin of his palm and the ulcers on the back. "You have the signs," he said.

"Signs? Of what?"

"The poison."

"But how . . ."

Hugh interrupted him. "It's time for justice," he said, standing up straight again. "Your turn to climb the ladders. Let's see how *you* fare."

Before Paul could object, Hugh had extinguished the oil lamp, enveloping Paul in blackness. The effect of being left alone in total darkness made Paul's blood run cold. "Hugh!" he cried. "No!"

Hugh did not reply. There was not even the sound of retreating footsteps. He had simply vanished.

Paul could not see his own hand in front of his face. In terror he called out, "Help! Help!" But it was useless. He was alone.

Feeling the slimy walls with his itching hands, he rose to his feet. Continuing to reach up, he touched the low ceiling that bore down on him. It was like a tomb. But it was no use grieving. He had to find the ladder. Sweeping his arms to and fro in front of him, he took a tentative step along the passage. He knew that he could be going in the wrong direction but he had to go somewhere. He took another couple of steps before his right arm touched something. Not rock or earth, it was damp wood. A post. Probably, Paul thought, a prop to support the ceiling. The wood, though, was crumbling. Next to the old prop, Paul could feel netting hanging against the wall. Perhaps, before it rotted, it protected the workers from falling rocks. He doubted that it was still strong enough to protect him if any rock should break free now.

Four more slow, cautious steps and Paul trod on something loose. Startled by the painful twisting of his ankle as his foot slipped off the object, Paul yelled, "Ow!" The cry echoed down the empty tunnel. He crouched down and fumbled about on the floor until his fingers found a curved piece of metal, long and heavy, pointed at both ends. A pickaxe. Judging by the roughness of its surface, it was badly rusted. Its handle must have rotted away altogether. He tossed it aside angrily. When it struck the wall, the deathly silence gave way to an unbearable racket. Instantly, a wooden support creaked and collapsed, sending a boom along the cave. The sound was followed by a cascade of rocks, as noisy as a burst of gunfire.

"Oh, no!" Paul exclaimed.

Despite the utter blackness, he jumped to his feet and ran. He had only gone a few paces when his left foot slammed into something. He wailed as he tripped over it, landing in a heap in a pool of dirty water.

The avalanche of rocks and earth continued to thunder for a few seconds then, mercifully, ceased.

Paul did not rise. He broke down and cried in desperation. "This is impossible," he whimpered. He wanted to blame someone – anyone – for his predicament. His parents, for bringing him to this horrible place. His uncaring ancestors, for managing the mine so cruelly. Hugh, for tormenting him in a crazy attempt at revenge. Even the punishment being inflicted on him was underhand. "It's not fair," Paul grumbled aloud. "I bet Thomas had a lamp at least." He buried his head in his hands. He was ready to give up.

Then, above his sobs, he heard another noise. Footsteps! Hugh must be coming back, he thought. His hunger for reprisal had been satisfied. He'd gloated enough over Paul's discomfort and now would return him to the surface.

Paul looked up. It was not the diffuse ball of light from Hugh's lamp that he saw approaching, but torchlight flashing

193

up and down, panning from side to side. The effect was eerie. Even though the arrival of the devil himself would have been a welcome relief from solitude, he dared not call out. Mesmerised by the swaying beam, he sat and waited, holding his breath.

The bright light touched him and stung his eyes. He recoiled, putting a hand up to shield them.

"What you be doing here?" asked the voice behind the torch.

Paul hesitated, then replied, "Is that you, Thomas?"

"Yes."

"Thank God." He added, "But you're . . ."

Thomas interrupted, repeating, "What you be doing here?"

"Your dad," Paul began unsteadily. "He . . . er . . ."

"I know my pa. I know what he's doing," said Thomas. "I mean, why are you *here*? Ladder's the other way." He flashed the torch beam in the direction from which Paul had come.

"I didn't know," Paul mumbled miserably.

Thomas looked down at Paul as if he were a wounded and defenceless animal. "You be in trouble. But I'll help, because you were kind to me. And," he said, offering Paul his hand, "the first thing I can learn you is not to sit yourself against boxes of gunpowder."

"What?" Paul exclaimed, grabbing the youngster's hand and yanking himself to his feet.

"Gunpowder. In the box."

The light picked out a decrepit old crate that Paul had tripped over.

"Come on," Thomas said coolly. "Walk round it this way. I know this place. You be safe with me."

Paul stopped staring at the box and followed the boy.

"But if we've got to get out this way," he said to his young guide, "we're trapped. There was a landslide."

"So I see," Thomas replied, examining the heap of rocks by torchlight. "Things always was bad here. Always falls. But this ain't so bad. We can climb over. Keep your head down, though. There ain't much room. Don't bump into anything else," he announced nonchalantly, "or you'll have the whole lot come down on us. Follow me."

On knees and forearms, Thomas scampered up and over the pile of debris. Paul, hating and hurting every inch of the way, followed suit.

Thomas was through the gap and back on his feet before Paul had got half way over the mound. Tired, Paul lay still for a moment and wiped his brow with a filthy sleeve. "Ugh!" he groaned. "This is awful. How could anyone survive down here, never mind work in these conditions?"

The boy smiled and shrugged. "We did. It was our life."

Paul felt like sobbing again, this time on Thomas's behalf, but he tried not to indulge in pity. After all, it was too late for remorse. It was pointless to tell Thomas that he'd been born too early, to the wrong family. "You must be tough," Paul said through the small hole.

"We was," Thomas responded quietly. "Now you must be tough as well. Keep coming. It's not good to take too long. And don't talk too loud. You could bring more rocks down on yourself."

Paul needed no further encouragement. He squirmed awkwardly through the gap under the ceiling then rolled, out of control, down the other side. He landed at Thomas's feet.

"That be one way of doing it quick," Thomas said. "Bet it hurt."

"Yes," Paul rejoined. "But I didn't have much choice." He did not have Thomas's agility.

Thomas helped him up again, saying, "Not far, then we start the climb up through the four seams. Two hours and you'll be home."

"Two hours!" Paul moaned. It seemed like an eternity. He really didn't know if he was capable of hauling himself up ladders for two hours. It would have been difficult even if he'd been fit.

Thomas seemed to sense his anxiety. "Don't worry. There be rest places every now and again."

The tunnel opened out into a chamber. The torchlight picked out a dilapidated truck, water streaming down the walls, and discarded tools.

"Look," Thomas said, pointing with the flashlight. "The bottom of the shaft."

Together the boys crossed the underground hall and looked up at the shaft. There was nothing to see but the iron steps extending vertically upwards. Paul shivered. "It's a long way up," he groaned. His head swam and his stomach churned. He vomited.

"You have the signs," Thomas murmured sadly.

"I'm afraid so," Paul replied, sinking into hopelessness.

"I did it once when I was like you," Thomas encouraged him. "Well," he admitted, "I almost made it."

Paul sighed. He glanced upwards once more and said, "Let's get on with it. It's going to be tough but I guess it beats rotting in this hellhole."

Thomas perked up. "Come on, then," he said, fixing the torch to his belt to free both his hands for the ascent. "I'll lead the way."

With the glow from the torch bobbing above him, Paul mounted the ladder and began the long slow slog. Thomas's young but experienced voice drifted down the dark shaft, "Don't look up or down while you be climbing. Just look straight ahead."

197

Some of the iron rungs were flat and wide enough to be comfortable on the feet. Where the original rungs had corroded, they had been replaced by round bars that felt less secure and dug painfully into Paul's soles through his trainers. At intervals, the ladder was fixed firmly into the rock so at least it did not flex unnervingly as he climbed.

"Slow down a bit," Paul called. The light had grown dim as Thomas's small muscular legs carried him upwards at a cracking pace.

"All right," he returned. "Soon be at level three."

Paul yanked on the ladder and clumsily raised one leg after the other. Before long he sighted Thomas, who was standing triumphantly on a ledge at the top of the first ladder. "Welcome to the third seam," he said cheerfully.

A little breathless, Paul dragged himself up into the tunnel, which looked just like the one below. He was grateful for a short break from the monotonous movement – hand over hand, left leg up, right leg up.

"Next ladder," Thomas said, still fresh. "Have a care on this one," he advised. "It's been repaired a lot. All sorts of rungs. Some wooden ones. They ain't so strong as they used to be. Count the rungs. The fifth and twelfth is missing."

Some way up the ladder, Thomas let out a small yell and bits of wood showered down on Paul's head and arms. "What's up?" Paul called to his young friend.

"Another rung just broke," he explained. "I'll climb up a bit, then shine the light on the broken one till you get past it. Yes?"

"Okay," Paul replied.

Concentrating more on the missing rung than on getting safely to it, Paul lifted his right leg and banged his knee. "Ow!" he squawked. Immediately he came to a standstill and waited for the pain to subside. Hooking himself to the ladder with one arm, he rubbed at his bruised knee with the free hand.

Thomas sounded concerned. "Are you all right? My knees are used to it. Kneecaps like armour. You being a Pengelly, you ain't so used to the knocks. It'll hurt at first."

"You're not kidding."

"If you stay still it'll get stiff. Best to keep going."

"Easier said than done," Paul replied. "You're probably right, though." Wincing at the pangs from his knee, he resumed the climb.

After a few more metres, being careful not to come a cropper at the missing rung, his knee began to move more freely and the twinges became less severe. But, by then, a relentless ache had set in his shoulders and calves.

When he heaved himself up onto the next level, he did not even try to get to his feet. "Let me sit and rest for a bit," he said.

Thomas shook his head sadly. "A long way to go yet."

"I know," Paul replied, still getting his breath back. "But as you said, we Pengellys aren't really fit enough for this."

"Just a minute or two," Thomas conceded, parking himself on a disused cart.

Paul knew what Thomas was, but as he flashed the beam playfully along the tunnel and swung his legs happily, he looked so real. It was as if his good deed in rescuing Paul gave meaning to his continuing existence.

"Thomas," Paul muttered, "I'm sorry about . . . what happened to you."

"It's all right," the boy replied. "That Christmas, I really wanted a present. Knew I wouldn't get one. So I was daft. But now . . ." He pointed to Paul's torch. "Now I got a real beauty."

Paul smiled at him. Smiled at the simple pleasure. He himself was expecting an expensive video game system, but he probably wouldn't experience the same thrill that Thomas had got out of a cheap torch and a bit of kindness.

"Ready to go on?" Thomas prompted. "There ain't nothing to worry about with the ladder to the first seam."

When he stood, Paul found that his wounded knee had stiffened a lot. He walked a short distance down the passageway and back to the foot of the ladder before attempting to climb. All the time he scratched at the back of his itching hands, opening up fresh sores and ripping the scabs off those that were healing. He couldn't help it. The irritation had become unbearable.

The ascent to level one was not particularly arduous but halfway up, Paul began to feel dizzy. He clung to the ladder, not daring to move till the bout of nausea had passed. When he felt a little stronger, he glanced back to gauge their progress. It was a mistake. He took one look at the apparently bottomless shaft and straight away began to retch.

Shining the light on him, Thomas remarked, "If you be queasy, don't look down."

"Too late." Paul wiped his mouth and tried to swallow the foul taste. After a moment, he said, "Okay. Let's get moving again."

"You be doing well," Thomas complimented him.

"It doesn't feel like it," Paul rejoined. His exertions and the sickness had brought on a sweat. He had to be careful to grip the ladder in case the moisture on his palms loosened his hold.

When they reached the first seam, Paul bent over, hands on knees, and spat the sourness from his mouth. "Ugh!" he moaned. Then he stretched himself and stood upright again.

"Better?" Thomas asked.

"A bit," Paul replied.

"No more seams," Thomas said. "Just a long climb. It ain't too bad, but be careful. In places, water runs down the left stile."

"Stile? What's that?"

"This." Thomas put his hand on the vertical part of the ladder that supported the treads. "The water makes it slippery. Keep over to the right side and hold onto the rungs when you climb. Don't use the stile or you'll lose your grip."

As he followed Thomas up the ladder, Paul realised how tired he was. To keep going he had to flog his weary muscles, ignore the agony in his knee and try to forget that he felt very sick. His clothes were drenched, not just with the water in the mine but also with sweat. Yet his greatest battle was with his willpower. He was not sure that he could match the determination Thomas had once shown.

Paul called to him, "Let's take a rest. I'm exhausted."

"There be a ledge up here a bit."

Thomas helped him to swing from the ladder into the recess cut in the wall. Straightaway he plonked himself down. Gasping for air, Paul looked up at Thomas and said, "I don't think I can make it."

"There's plenty of ledges. You can stop and get your strength back."

"What strength?"

Thomas tried to console him. "I know," he said. "It's . . . hard. But what else can you do?"

"Nothing," Paul admitted. He put his hand on the stile to pull himself up, but it was like trying to grip a greasy pole. "You're right," he said to Thomas. "It *is* slippery."

Paul knew that he was climbing much slower than before. He could not help it. He felt so weak. Even short distances between the resting places seemed to take him an age to cover. In spite of taking longer and longer breaks, he had not recovered from one climb before he started the next. He was sick once more before Thomas asked, "Can you feel it?"

"What?"

"Air."

"Air? Fresh air?" Paul breathed in deeply and concentrated. "No."

"The air be fresher. And there be a breeze."

"Really?" Paul sensed nothing. Looking up, he could not see the night sky. "You're just saying that to make me feel better."

"No," Thomas replied. "It's not so far now. You *can* make it."

Paul sighed and, taking Thomas's hand, let the boy tug him to his feet. While Thomas mounted the ladder, Paul rubbed at his gritty eyes to clear his vision. His sight was still blurred when he clasped the ladder. He took hold of a rung with his right hand but his left slipped on the wet stile. In a frenzied attempt to find purchase with his feet, his legs kicked at one rung and then another. Both treads snapped and fell down the shaft with an ominous clatter. Paul screeched. He held onto the ladder by his right hand. His legs flailed about uselessly. "Help!" he yelled hysterically.

Thomas shouted back, "Grip with your other hand! Bring your legs up to the next rung."

But Paul was in shock. He was so scared that he could not hear. Dangling over the void, he clutched desperately at his lifeline with one hand, unable to do more to save himself.

"Hang on!" Thomas called. "I'm coming."

Thomas was small enough to ease himself round the edge of the ladder and into the narrow gap between the wall of earth and the rungs. He descended on the inside of the ladder till he drew level with Paul. He caught hold of Paul's left hand and forcibly placed it on a rung. Then he went down further. Clinging carefully to the ladder with one hand, he grabbed one of Paul's legs firmly to stop it thrashing about. He bent the knee upwards and directed the foot onto a secure rung.

Feeling something solid underneath him, Paul snapped out of his panic and lodged his other foot on the same rung. Suddenly safe, he groaned and wept.

Squeezing past on the inside, Thomas said, "You be all right now. You can get going again."

"I can't move," Paul replied, tears running down his face. "I can't."

"You can!" Thomas swung himself back onto the ledge so that he was not in danger of falling himself. "You have to!" he implored.

"My legs won't move!"

"So what are you going to do?" Thomas exclaimed. "Stay here till you drop?"

"I don't know," Paul whimpered.

In exasperation, Thomas replied, "You Pengellys *are* soft. I'm going on. And I'm taking the torch. If you want the light you'll *have* to come after me."

Nimbly, Thomas mounted the ladder again and began to clamber up.

"No!" Paul shouted after him. "Don't leave me in the dark!"

The young lad carried on climbing. "Follow me then," he called.

Slowly, Paul regained his nerve. His dread of the dark was greater than his fear of falling. He dared to unclench his fist from one rung and snatch at the next. He dragged one leg unwillingly from its foothold to the higher rung. His muscles strained once more and, inch by inch, he lugged himself up. At each rung, he paused and sighed.

Way above him, like a guardian angel, Thomas called out,

"Don't stop! Keep going. It's the only way. No more rests, just keep coming steady."

Paul did not have the energy to respond. He struggled upwards as best as he could. Thomas waited patiently as Paul eventually caught up with him. Paul took comfort in being closer to the light and tried his hardest to keep going at a reasonable pace.

At one point, he did stop. He couldn't help himself. "Thomas!" he shouted. "I *can* smell it. Fresh air!"

"That's right," Thomas replied. "Don't look up but you can see the stars from here. Not long now."

"Stars," Paul muttered gratefully as if he were discovering them for the first time. With renewed spirit, he resumed the ascent.

They were close to the open air but it still took Paul fifteen minutes of pure agony to reach it. His fingers were so numb from the damp and cold metal that they could hardly feel to grip. His body was feverishly hot and his head ached alarmingly. The raw soles of his feet smarted each time they trod on another rung and, with each step up, his knee stung. His breath came in short, painful gasps.

Above him, Thomas let out a cry of delight. "We've made it! I'm climbing out, Paul. You're nearly there!"

Steeling himself, Paul looked up and saw Thomas's face peering down at him from the safety of the lawn and, beyond, a beautiful night sky. He could even feel a reassuring breeze on his own face. "Great!"

"Don't rush at it," Thomas advised. "Just take it easy. Keep coming at your own pace. Don't you be careless now."

"Okay." But Paul could not resist speeding up for the last few metres. He was desperate to escape from the dark shaft. He risked grips that before he would have changed at least twice before trusting. He tried to calm himself when one foot slipped unexpectedly off a rung. He stopped and mumbled to himself, "Careful."

Then, above him, he heard a commotion. Thomas was being lifted bodily from the edge of the shaft and put to one side.

"You shouldn't have helped him, Thomas," Hugh's angry voice yelled. "He's a Pengelly."

"I know. But . . ."

"No buts," his father shouted. "This be the night for the Pengellys to know what it's like."

"He knows, Pa. He's suffered enough."

"Not yet he hasn't."

Hugh looked down the hole at Paul and smirked. He glanced back at his son and said, "He's finished. Just like you were."

"But he can make it!"

"No, he won't. He's only got this far because you helped him. He gets no further."

Hugh, seeming to be as alive and solid as Paul's own father, reached down to the ladder and pushed and pulled it to loosen it from its anchorage.

"No!" Paul and Thomas cried at the same time.

Thomas grabbed hold of his father. "It wasn't his fault, Pa!" he shouted.

"Leave me be!" Hugh ordered. He pushed Thomas away roughly.

Standing up, Hugh lifted his big old boot, then slammed it down on the top of the ladder.

Paul screamed as the ladder jolted free of its fixtures. It lurched and sagged. Paul clung tightly as it wobbled in the air.

Above him, Hugh murmured, "This time." He swung his leg with all his might at the top of the wrecked ladder.

The kick never found its mark. The ground gave way underneath him and he toppled into the dark shaft.

By instinct Paul lunged at Hugh in an attempt to grasp and save him, but the ladder swung away and he was clutching at thin air. All he could do was listen to Hugh's wail that receded terrifyingly quickly.

His arms hooked round the rungs, Paul swayed from one side of the shaft to the other on the loose ladder.

Picking himself off the grass, Thomas crawled to the edge of the hole and looked down in disbelief. "Pa!" he cried.

There was no response.

Paul called up to him. "Thomas! I'm sorry. I couldn't catch him."

When he saw Paul's plight, Thomas gathered his wits. He peered round the garden. Catching sight of the rope that had been part of the fence, he grabbed a length of it. Making a loop in the cord, he threw it over the top of the ladder and pulled, forcing the ladder to the edge of the shaft.

"All right," he shouted to Paul. "You come up. I'll hold it against the side."

The ladder rocked but did not spring back to its mid-air position. After a few minutes, Paul's white face emerged from the shaft and he scrambled onto firm ground. Thomas let go of the rope.

The two boys stood for an instant, looked at each other, then came together in an embrace. One sobbed with relief, the other with grief.

After a while, Paul pulled away and put his hands on Thomas's shoulders. "What now?" he asked.

Thomas wiped his eyes and replied, "You go and get fixed up. You've proved you ain't so soft – for a Pengelly – but you still need a doctor."

"Yes," Paul agreed. "But what about you?"

"I don't belong here."

"How do you mean?"

"This ain't my world. I belong down there. With my pa."

"But . . ."

It was too late. Thomas had squirmed out of his grasp, dashed across the lawn and leapt onto the ladder that swayed in the void. He made no attempt to grip the rungs. Instead he took hold of the slippery sides of the ladder and slid rapidly down the shaft, out of Paul's view.

Paul crept as close as he dared to the hole and whispered into it, "You didn't even give me time to thank you." He shook his head then called into the abyss, "Thanks, Thomas!"

He stood up, groaning at the pain, and staggered towards the back door. He did not make it. He collapsed before he reached the safety of the house.

It was Christmas Day. Paul slept soundly, recovering from his ordeal. When the doctor arrived, he was not alone. He had with him Detective Superintendent Challis and a team of police officers. Superintendent Challis talked to Paul's father while his team scoured the property and the doctor chatted with Mrs Pengelly.

"Let me read you a list of symptoms," the GP said to her. "See what you think. Okay?"

Mrs Pengelly nodded.

"Nervousness, thirst, vomiting, hallucinations, thickening of the skin on the soles and palms, cyanosis. That's a blue coloration," he explained. "Irritation of the hands and eyes, skin ulceration, tanned skin, collapse."

Paul's mother swallowed. "Yes. That's Paul all right. What does it mean?"

"That's an old list of the symptoms of arsenic poisoning."

"Poisoning!" she exclaimed.

"I had my suspicions earlier. The tests confirmed it. Paul has a lot of arsenic in his body."

"Where could it have come from?" his mother asked, still stunned by the news.

"It's not at dangerous levels in these parts. Not outside the old mines, anyway. So it's not from natural contamination. That's why I informed the police. It was in your tomato sauce. In other words, it was a deliberate attempt to poison Paul."

Mrs Pengelly stared at the doctor. Her mouth was open but no words would come out.

Outside, Detective Superintendent Challis turned to Paul's dad and asked, "This workshop, Mr Pengelly. Who's been in it?"

211

"No one. Why?"

"Are you sure?"

"Yes. No one but me. I dumped all my stuff in it and locked it up."

"So you're the only one who could possibly have been in it?" the policeman checked.

"Yes. Why?"

"Mr Pengelly, what's this?" He held up a jar that one of his team had found when they broke into the shed.

"A jar. I keep nails in it."

"It's definitely yours, is it?"

"Yes."

Donning gloves, the policeman unscrewed the top and peered inside. "Nails, eh?" He tilted the jar towards Mr Pengelly and asked, "How do you explain this, then?"

The jar was half full of a white powder.

"I don't know. What is it?"

"The lab will confirm it in due course, but we have reason to believe it's arsenic."

"Arsenic?"

"Arsenic trioxide, to be precise. And your son has acute arsenic poisoning from eating tomato sauce that's been tampered with. Your GP tells me that Paul's the only one around here who eats tomato sauce. Convenient, eh? And you're the only one with access to this little store of arsenic."

"You don't think . . ."

"What else should I think?"

"But I didn't . . . I couldn't . . ."

"Mr Pengelly," the detective announced, "I charge you with the attempted murder of your son." He turned to his deputy and said, "Read him his rights and take him away."

On the lawn, the scar began to heal. The malice that had opened the old sore was exhausted. The earth compressed the dark shaft, reclaiming the land and concealing all evidence that it had ever existed.

HOME FOR CHRISTMAS

David Belbin

hristmas Eve was not a good day to hitch-hike. Billy had been at the Services for nearly five hours without a sniff of a lift. No-one had even slowed down to take a look at him. And the weather was lousy. At one point, he'd had to shelter from the rain next to some bins behind the petrol station. He'd dozed off, and there was another hour gone.

Now it was getting dark, and a fog was coming in. Cars drove by him as if he wasn't there. So much for Christmas spirit! It wasn't as though Billy had a big, off-putting bag either. All he carried was a small knapsack, which used to belong to his mum. It contained all his worldly goods, such as they were, and would fit beneath his legs in the smallest car.

Maybe he should cross the six-lane road, and try to hitch back to London, where he'd come from that morning. People said that you could get a bed and something to eat more easily at Christmas. But no. With Billy's luck, he'd probably get run over crossing the motorway.

Billy began to cough. He'd had this cold on and off for two months. Other dossers told him that your body got used to the life, when you'd been living on the streets long enough. Maybe. He'd been sleeping rough for a year now. That was long enough for him to decide that it wasn't the life for him.

The fog was getting thicker. It was colder, too. When it got really dark, he'd wander into the Happy Eater, warm up a bit. Billy had enough money left for a cup of coffee. That was, presuming they'd serve him. He looked a mess.

The rain started up again. Billy shivered. His anorak was supposed to be "shower-proof", but it was wet through. Puddles were forming around his feet. Suddenly, he saw a lorry, coming towards him from the direction of the petrol station. The lorry didn't have its lights on and was driving really close to the kerb. Instead of holding his thumb out, Billy took a step back. He didn't want to get splashed by the foul, oily water that lay on the road.

Still, the lorry seemed to be driving straight at him. Billy decided to get out of its way. But as he was about to make his move, the lorry turned its lights on, full beam. He couldn't see a thing. He stood there, frozen to the spot, like a rabbit blinded by the poacher's torch, waiting to be shot.

The lorry stopped. One of its wheels was on the kerb, only centimetres from Billy's right foot. The passenger door opened. A deep, guttural voice spoke.

"You after a lift?"

It all felt wrong. Billy knew that. But it was raining hard now, and he had been at the Services all day. He went up to the door and opened it a little farther.

"How far are you going?" the deep voice asked.

Billy still couldn't see the driver, only hear his harsh Glaswegian accent.

"I'm going to Scotland. To Gretna."

"I'm going that way myself. Get in."

Billy hesitated. He had learnt to walk away from threatening situations. But the man was Scottish, like him, and could take him all the way home—or, at least, to the place he used to call home.

Billy got into the cabin. He slid his bag beneath his feet and pulled on the seatbelt before looking at the driver.

"Thanks for stopping," he said. "It's pretty horrible out there."

The man said nothing. His thick hands reached for the gear stick. He began to accelerate onto the M1, towards the grim, frozen north.

In the half light of the lorry cabin, Billy looked at the driver. The man was in his late thirties, forty at most. He had short, dark hair which was in an even worse condition than his own. It looked like wire wool. The man's eyes were set so deeply beneath his heavy eyebrows that Billy could barely make them out. His face was pock-marked and scarred, except for where a thick moustache covered his upper lip. He was heavy set, and wore a lumberjack shirt over shapeless jeans.

Billy hadn't done a lot of hitching, but he knew that there was an etiquette. The hitcher had to make conversation. It was your duty to entertain the driver, even if he didn't have a lot to say for himself. The driver had to concentrate on the driving, after all.

"I'm Billy," he said to the man, in his friendliest voice, "Billy Gates."

For a moment, he thought that the driver wasn't going to reply.

"Hank."

"Bad day to have to work, Christmas Eve."

Again, Hank didn't answer. Instead, he speeded up, until they were doing fifty. The fog was getting thicker and it felt too fast. Still, it wasn't Billy's place to say their speed was dangerous.

The silence was almost as threatening as the speed they

were doing. There was a radio. B.
should suggest switching it on.

"Should I . . .?"

Hank interrupted before Billy had form

"I don't like music."

The way he said it made Billy want to jump ош of the cab, even though their speed was up to fifty-five and there was nothing but filthy fog outside. Instead, he began to say the first things that came into his mind.

"The radio would probably be all carols and that kind of stuff," he said. "I hate that soppy, sentimental attitude at Christmas—trying to make it sound like all men are brothers. It's not true, is it? I mean, do you know how many cars went by before you picked me up?"

Hank remained silent.

"A thousand at least."

Now that he'd started talking, he couldn't stop.

"I think Christmas is a pain, really," Billy said. "You know what I mean? Everyone's expected to have a good time, so when you're not, somehow it seems a hundred times worse."

"Aye," said Hank. "I know that all right."

He began to drive even faster.

*　　*　　*

fog kept coming and going. It was easy to see how pile-ups happened in weather like this. Just when you thought you were clear, another dense patch would hit you. Hank didn't seem to care. He drove right up to the car in front, forcing it to speed up or change lanes. Then, just as Billy thought they were bound to collide, Hank slammed on the brakes. They missed by centimetres.

Hank did this several times. Obviously, he enjoyed flirting with death. Billy spent most of the journey on the edge of his seat, trying to convince himself that he was going to survive the ride. They were doing sixty now, and, as they reached the M6, there were fewer other cars on the road. Billy began to worry about black ice.

"Are you going home for Christmas?" Billy asked.

"You could say that," Hank replied.

Billy's stomach rumbled. He hadn't eaten all day.

"I'm looking forward to Christmas dinner," Billy said, thinking aloud.

He hoped his dad had enough food in for two.

"Aye, Christmas dinner," Hank said. "I"m looking forward to that myself."

"Roast turkey," Billy said, like the words were a prayer or an incantation. "With roast potatoes and brussels sprouts. Bread sauce."

Hank grinned, revealing a missing tooth.

"I love to carve," he said, then added, darkly, "know what I mean?"

"Yes," Billy replied, though he didn't, really.

The driver turned back to the road. Fog gave way to heavy rain. Hank drove even faster, making Billy tense up. Then, when the needle hit seventy, Hank stopped accelerating. He seemed to sense Billy's relief.

"Can't go over seventy," he explained, almost apologetically. "Lorry's fitted with a tachograph, records the distance and speed you've done."

"What are you carrying?" Billy asked, relieved about the speed.

Hank didn't answer.

"It's none of my business," Billy said. "Sorry."

Hank said nothing. But a minute later, he asked Billy a question.

"Why're you going to Gretna?"

"I'm going home for Christmas," Billy told him. "Well, for good, really. I went down to London but things didn't work out for me there. So I decided to see if my dad'll take me back, catch up with my mates, go back to school even."

"Aye," said Hank. "You want to go to school, get an education. You wouldn't catch me doing what I'm doing today if I'd had an education."

For a moment Hank's voice had been warm, almost

paternal, but then the Glaswegian resumed his silence. He kept driving at a steady seventy, through the wind and rain. Billy had been with him for nearly five hours. They weren't far from Scotland, now. Suddenly Hank spoke again.

"You haven't said what made you leave in the first place."

Billy hesitated before answering. His fear of Hank had abated. If the driver had meant to harm him, he could have done so hours ago. He decided to trust Hank. After all, he *had* given him a lift. None of the well-dressed people in their posh cars had stopped. Hank couldn't help it if he looked so threatening. That was just the way he was. Come to think of it, Billy probably looked a bit threatening himself.

"It was my dad," he told Hank, in a quiet voice. "He always drank a lot. He knocked my mum about, too. But when she was alive, she stopped him from really hurting me. Then she got cancer . . ."

He paused. He hadn't realised how much it would hurt him to talk about it.

"The night after the funeral he nearly broke both my legs. After that, it was every day. When he wasn't hitting me he was shouting at me. He wasn't stupid either. He didn't leave marks. Once, I told someone at school about it. I thought being taken into care would be better than living with him. But he convinced them that I was making it up, because I blamed him for my mum's death. They made me see a psychiatrist instead.

"Last Christmas was OK, at first. My gran—my mother's mum, she's the only grandparent I've got—she came out of the old people's home to spend Christmas dinner with us. But when Dad got back from driving her home, he was in a foul mood. He started drinking, then he started throwing things about. He blacked both my eyes. I could hardly see. Then he passed out. I took all the money I could find in the house and as many things as I could cram into this bag here and cleared off."

Most people, Billy thought, would have made some sympathetic comment after this speech. Hank said nothing.

It was after ten now. Billy realised that it would be the early hours of the morning before he got to Gretna. He didn't want to wake his dad up. Still, one more night sleeping in a cold doorway wouldn't hurt him.

"Why are you going back to him?" Hank asked, five minutes later, in a voice that was almost sympathetic.

Billy took a deep breath before replying.

"Because there's nowhere else to go. Because I've met people on the streets whose parents did far, far worse things to them, worse than I could have imagined when I ran away. Because if I don't sort out my past, I won't have a future.

And because my dad had his reasons, too. Mum died. He was made redundant. I was the only person to take it out on. Maybe a year on his own will have been good for him. Who knows, maybe he'll be glad to see me."

Hank made a noise which was half way between a grunt and an ironic laugh.

"And if he isn't?"

"I'm still only fifteen. If my dad won't take me in, the council would have to put me somewhere. No matter how bad it turns out to be, it couldn't be worse than the last two months have been."

The road was nearly empty. To Billy's surprise, Hank began to slow down.

"What are you doing?"

Hank pulled into a deserted Services. The restaurant and petrol station were both closed.

"Why have we stopped? Are you tired?"

Hank shook his head.

"It's the law. I've been driving eight hours, so I have to have eight hours' rest before I can carry on. If I don't, the tachograph will show me up and I'll be in trouble."

He looked out at the road.

"You can have a go at hitching another lift if you want,

224

though I doubt you'll be lucky." Seeing the dubious look in Billy's eyes, he added, "Don't worry, I'll have you home before tomorrow morning's over. You'll get your precious Christmas dinner."

"Thanks."

Hank got out of his driver's seat, then made himself a bed in the bunk at the back of the cabin. Billy put his seat as far back as it would go, which wasn't far, then he tried to sleep.

It wasn't easy. He was wide awake. He kept thinking about his father and whether what Hank had hinted was right—whether it was a mistake to go back.

Eventually, Billy ran out of things to worry about. He was beginning to doze when a noise startled him. It was Hank, talking. At first Billy couldn't make out what the driver was saying.

"Pardon?"

No reply. Billy closed his eyes. Hank spoke again.

"I'll cut his heart out," Hank announced, in a deep, threatening voice, "while you watch. And then I'll cut out yours."

Hank was talking in his sleep. It gave Billy the creeps. Nevertheless, he tried to sleep. The voice wasn't deliberate, after all. Hank was just having a nightmare. Billy knew all about those.

Now that the engine had been turned off, the cabin was

cold. The seat was uncomfortable, too. Billy's anorak had dried off, but he'd already caught a chill. He decided to get the spare sweater out of his bag. As he reached down beneath his seat, Hank spoke again, in a scary, unnatural voice.

"Having your Christmas dinner, are you? Shall I carve?" Then he laughed, loudly—a fierce, demonic laugh.

That was it. Billy could no longer pretend to himself that he wasn't scared. As quietly as he could manage, Billy opened the cabin door. As he stepped onto cold tarmac, closing the door behind him, he heard the driver cackle again, in a chilling parody of an American accent.

"Hi honey, I'm home!"

If I stayed in that truck, Billy thought, I'd be a dead man.

With luck, Billy would be able to hitch away from here. Drivers were more generous in the north than in the south, after all. It was a busy motorway; there had to be some traffic.

To get to the road, he had to pass the end of Hank's lorry. It was deathly quiet. However, as Billy walked by the back of the lorry, he could hear a distinct humming noise coming from inside. Billy didn't know what it was, but he knew that he had to get away as quickly as possible. He stood anxiously by the slip road.

It was very dark. No cars passed. Even if they did, they

were unlikely to pause by a closed service station. The terrible cold made Billy shiver. Thinking about how he'd spent seven hours with a psychopath made him shiver even more.

Still no cars passed. Despite the sleep he'd had at the Services earlier, Billy was terribly tired. He hadn't eaten. Neither, he realised, had Hank, in all the hours they'd spent together. Hunger added to Billy's tiredness. He considered walking, but had no idea how far he was from any kind of town. And he was so tired. All he had to do was curl up somewhere and sleep until it was light, until Hank had gone. When he awoke, the driver would assume that Billy had got another lift, and that would be the end of it.

Billy walked to the small, self-service restaurant and looked around. He needed to find a spot out of the wind which was tearing around the building. His best bet was a bin area, like the one he'd slept in earlier. Soon he found it: a huge waste bin, surrounded by bags of refuse. Billy looked inside. He was in luck. The bin had been emptied, and there was a fresh plastic bag inside.

Billy got in. It was a bit smelly but he'd slept in worse. He got out his sweater, to use as a pillow, then he pulled the heavy plastic around him, so that it acted as a kind of sleeping bag. There were vents on the side of the bin. He wouldn't suffocate. And Hank would never find him here. Feeling safe at last, Billy drifted off into a dreamless sleep.

When Billy woke it was morning, but he had no idea of the time. It took him a couple of minutes to remember where he was. Noises from the restaurant helped him to work it out. Hank and the long lorry journey seemed like a nightmare. Billy felt in his pockets. He still had a little money. Things were cheaper in the north. Maybe he'd be able to afford tea and toast. He needed it. He was starving.

Billy lifted the bin lid off. His limbs were stiff, and it took him a couple of goes to get out. Outside, there was a morning mist. Shiny, white smoke seemed to float around Billy, making the landscape seem unreal. He could hardly make out the dark silhouette of the restaurant building, never mind anything beyond it. Useless weather for hitching. But never mind. Maybe he'd be able to cadge a lift from someone inside the restaurant.

The place was more like a transport caff than a motorway restaurant. It was warm, though. There were three men sitting at tables. All of them seemed to be drivers, like Hank. Maybe it wasn't so unusual to be working on Christmas Day.

"I'm surprised you're open," he said to a waitress, who was carrying over a cooked breakfast.

"Just till midday," she replied. "Most places don't, but some of our regulars have nowhere else to go."

Like me, Billy thought. The woman pointed at the Christmas menu chalked on a blackboard. Billy's mouth watered, but it was much more than he could afford. Billy walked up to the counter. Only as he got there, was he able to see the cashier's desk, hidden around a corner. Standing at it was Hank.

Under fluorescent lights, Hank looked even more threatening than he had in the lorry. His eyes were bloodshot and several of his teeth were missing. The driver gave Billy a leering grin.

"I wondered where you'd got to. I knew you wouldn't be far away. Come on, sit down. I've ordered yours."

Part of Billy wanted to run. But there was nowhere for him to go to. The other part of him hadn't eaten since yesterday morning. He was weak with hunger. Whatever Hank had ordered had to be better than anything the meagre change in Billy's pocket could buy.

"Thanks," Billy said.

"Where did you get to?" Hank asked, his voice lighter than the night before.

"Call of nature," Billy replied, not having time to think of a better lie.

He wondered if Hank believed him. How long ago had the driver woken up? Hank looked at his watch.

"They'd better get a move on," he said. "I need to be in Glasgow by twelve."

"What are you carrying?" Billy asked, trying to settle his mind. "I heard this humming noise from the back of the lorry."

"Aye," said Hank. "The refrigeration unit. You have to keep it ticking over. But I've nothing in the back. I'm on my way to pick up a load of fish to take back to London. There's a big rush on fish after Christmas, you know. All those people who've pigged out over the holiday. They want something lighter, less fatty."

Billy breathed a sigh of relief. This was the longest speech Hank had given since they'd met. The threatening edge had vanished from his voice. Maybe last night Hank was tired, cranky, not himself. After all, he couldn't help it if he had nightmares and talked in his sleep.

"Here you are," said the waitress, "our first of the day. Hope you two enjoy it. Merry Christmas!"

As Billy and Hank returned her greeting, she laid two plates in front of them: roast turkey, with roast potatoes and parsnips, brussels sprouts, mashed potatoes, carrots and lashings of gravy. Just looking at it, being able to smell it, made Billy want to cry with gratitude.

"No bread sauce," Hank apologised, "but there is cranberry." He passed the bottle to Billy.

"This is . . . really generous of you," Billy stuttered. "Amazing. Thank you."

"Aye, well . . . in case your father hasn't the food in for you. And . . . if he has, I'm sure you could eat the same meal twice."

Billy nodded, then began to stuff his face with food. It was the best Christmas dinner he'd ever tasted. He ate it far too quickly. Hank, too, seemed to have an appetite. Soon they were tucking into Christmas pudding with rum sauce, washed down with a big mug of coffee.

Back in the lorry, Billy remembered something.

"You'll be eating a second Christmas dinner too, won't you? You said last night you were looking forward to it."

Hank laughed, the same sinister laugh as the night before.

"I said that I was looking forward to carving," he told Billy. "I didn't say anything about eating as well."

The cab hadn't warmed up yet, and Billy shivered. But he wasn't as scared as he had been the night before. Some people, he realised had a macabre sense of humour. They made jokes which didn't quite add up. It didn't mean that they were about to chop you into little pieces.

With the meal inside him, Billy felt much better. All was

right with the world, for a while at least. And they didn't have far to go. The journey seemed to be hurrying by.

"Want a coffee?" Hank asked, as they sped past Penrith.

Billy looked at the road ahead. There were no Services in sight.

"I filled a thermos when we stopped," Hank told him. "It's in the cubby hole behind. You don't mind sharing a cup, d'you?"

"No, no."

Billy reached into the back of the cabin. He could see the thermos, its red top poking out of Hank's holdall. As he pulled it out, he saw something else, glinting from the darkness of the bag. Billy pushed the flap of the bag back. The object was a large meat cleaver, its edges scratched where it had been sharpened. Billy drew in breath.

"What's happened to the coffee?" Hank asked.

Billy opened the thermos slowly.

"Cat got your tongue?"

Billy was silent. Hank sighed.

"You've seen something you shouldn't, haven't you?"

Billy mumbled.

"I guess." He didn't dare look at Hank.

The driver began to laugh—a harsh laugh, like that of the man who'd talked in his sleep the night before. Then he spoke again.

"If you don't pour me some coffee, I'll be tempted to use that thing on you."

His hand shaking, Billy opened the thermos and tipped coffee into the cup, spilling some on his jeans. Trembling, he passed it to Hank, who drank as he drove. Both of his hands were occupied, Billy realised. He could take the cleaver now, force Hank to stop the lorry, let him out. All he had to do was reach round, quickly.

But he couldn't do it. The driver was far too intimidating. He would stop Billy somehow. What was it he'd said? *I love to carve.*

"Here, don't you want some?"

Billy took the cup and forced some sweet coffee down his throat. He felt ill now, barely alive. He knew he shouldn't have taken this ride in the first place. *Always trust your instincts.* He should have learnt that by now. But it was too late. He was already dead.

"It's all right, you know," Hank said with a laugh in his voice. "The chopper's not for you."

"Of course not," Billy said in a weak voice. "Why would it be?"

They had left the motorway now, and were driving past Carlisle. Hank laughed his hollow, nasty laugh.

"I've killed people before because I didn't like the way they looked at me," he said, "back in the Gorbals. But you're all right. I like you. You're safe with me."

Billy looked at Hank's face to see if he was lying. He saw only a twisted smile.

"You want to know what I'm doing with that thing?"

"Sure."

Whatever Hank said, Billy wouldn't believe him. People would say anything to get you to go with them, he knew that. From now on, his life was in mortal danger.

"I've spent the last five years inside," Hank told him. "Not for murder—I've done a few of those but they've never proved one. For G.B.H. Only a wee doing over, really, but the police gave the judge a good idea about what I'd got away with before, and he gave me the maximum sentence. I got out two days ago. The wife doesn't know yet."

"You must be looking forward to seeing her," Billy said, politely.

"Oh, I am that. Y'see, it was her who shopped me. Not that she gave evidence herself, oh no. It was her new bloke who put me in the frame. A grass. He told the police about a couple of killings I'd done, too—he got them from her—but they didn't stand up in court. They thought I'd do twenty years minimum. But here I am, five years later, with remission for good behaviour, on my way to visit them."

Billy saw what Hank was getting at.

"You're going to use that . . . that thing on them?"

Hank nodded.

"You're not going to tell me they don't deserve it? I pick up the fish at twelve, then I go over to my old place. You know what I'm gonna do? I'm going to tie her up, then I'm going to chop him into little pieces while she watches. Then, when I'm done, I'll do the same to her."

Billy shuddered, but he wasn't convinced. If the story were true, why would Hank be telling him it?

"The police are bound to know it was you," he told Hank.

Hank shrugged.

"Maybe. But they'll have a hard time proving it. There's half a dozen blokes who'll claim I was in the smoke with them at the weekend."

"But what about this lorry? Your job?"

Hank laughed.

"It's not my job. That's why I've had to be so careful with the speed limit and the rest times. I'm doing a favour for a mate who wanted Christmas off. Let's say it was to our mutual advantage."

"Even so," Billy said, still unsure whether Hank was winding him up, "you're bound to be the main suspect."

"Yes," said Hank, "there's a chance I'll be seen. But I'll park the lorry well away from the house, wear gloves and a balaclava. I'll take my chances. Maybe I'll do in someone else on the way back, make it look like there's one of those serial killers about."

"Er . . ." Billy shivered again. Hank smiled.

"No, not you, lad. Someone who deserves it."

They were approaching the turn-off for Gretna.

"You can drop me here," Billy said, urgently. "This is fine."

"Nonsense," said Hank. "You've got a cold. You've been coughing all the while. I'll take you to your door. Point the way."

Reluctantly, Billy did as he was told.

"You're not sure, are you," Hank said, "whether to believe me or not? You won't be sure until you read it in the papers."

"No," said Billy. "I guess I won't be."

"You could go to the police I suppose, as soon as you get home."

"I wouldn't do that," Billy said, though he had been thinking of it only a moment before.

"It wouldn't do any good. They'd laugh in your face. And if they believed you . . . what could they do? You don't know my real name or where I live. All you know about is the lorry."

Billy nodded. Hank went on.

"Afterwards, that's when you could shop me. But I'm a good judge of people. I don't think you will. I'll take my chances, anyway. Revenge, that's all I've lived for these last

236

five years. If they catch me, put me back inside for the rest of my life, I can take it. I'll have got what I wanted."

"Do you really think it'll make you feel better?" Billy asked.

Hank laughed his maniac's laugh.

"Maybe not," he cackled. "But it'll make them feel a whole lot worse!"

He pulled over to the side of the road.

"Which one is it?"

Billy pointed. The house was on its own, with a single light in the doorway.

"It looks like someone's home," Hank said.

"Yes."

"I hope he's happy to see you."

"So do I. Thanks for the lift."

For a moment, Billy thought that Hank was going to offer him his hand to shake, but the driver only grinned at him. Billy opened the passenger door and got out of the cabin as quickly as he could. With back turned, he walked away from the lorry, into the misty morning.

Behind him, he heard the lorry drive off. Billy realised that he'd left his bag in the cabin. Never mind. There was nothing in it that he much cared for.

Was Hank telling the truth? Was he on his way to murder two people in the most horrible way he could imagine?

Maybe. Probably. Billy didn't know. He wasn't sure of anything any more, least of all the welcome that awaited him at his father's house. Did people really change? Or was it only that they sometimes got better at hiding their true natures?

The house was in front of him. The light from the front room penetrated the mist. The house was exactly as Billy remembered it. All he had to do was lift the brass knocker and let it fall. But Billy hesitated. This wasn't his home any more, he realised that now. He belonged in another place.

The knock echoed through the house, but the answering footsteps were a long time coming. Eventually, a voice sounded: crabby, a little threatening, but not that of an ogre, not quite.

"Who is it?"

"The spirit of Christmas present."

A joke. Why not?

"Do I know you?"

The door opened. The man who answered it was sallow-faced, balding, about Hank's age.

"Your son."

"What?"

He smelt of drink. The whole house smelt of stale whisky and roasting turkey.

"I know your son."

Mr Gates frowned.

"From the police, are you?"

"What? No."

Mention of the police made Hank nervous. He held up the bag which Billy Gates had left in his cabin.

"Your son. I gave him a lift earlier. He left this in my lorry. I was on my way back, so I thought I'd drop by with it."

Brusquely, Mr Gates opened the door a bit further.

"You'd better come in."

Hank entered the house. There was no hallway. You walked straight into the cramped front room: dusty, damp, dark, in need of a woman's touch. Mr Gates lifted a bottle of scotch from the top of a T.V. which was broadcasting the Queen's speech with the sound down.

"Drink?"

Hank nodded. He pulled off his balaclava, then took the glass and downed the whisky in one go.

"Cheers!"

Billy's father refilled the glass, then picked up Billy's bag.

"Where's your son?" Hank asked.

Mr Gates didn't answer the question, merely turned the bag round and round in his hands.

"This was his all right. It belonged to my wife before him."

"Where *is* Billy?"

Mr Gates emptied the bag onto the bare floorboards. There wasn't much in it. Then he began to examine a photograph which showed a smiling blonde woman holding a baby. Hank began to worry. He remembered the delay in answering the door. Suppose Billy had taken his story seriously? Suppose the boy had left the house, gone off to fetch the police?

"You gave my son a lift, you say?" Mr Gates asked, putting the photograph down.

"That's right," Hank said.

"Yesterday, was it?"

"Yes."

Mr Gates looked confused.

"If you were coming to Scotland, why did you not bring him with you? Why did you leave him at those Services outside London?"

"I didn't leave him there," Hank replied, wondering what was going on. "That was where I picked him up."

Mr Gates frowned. Hank didn't like him. He reminded him of one of the warders in prison, one of the more sadistic ones.

"And when did you drop him?"

"Three hours ago."

Mr Gates should have known that. Something was wrong, Hank realised. He'd wanted to see Billy again, to remind himself of the one good thing he'd done recently, before he got back into his cabin and returned to hell. But it didn't feel right. Hank stood.

"Give Billy my regards. I have to be on my way now."

"On Christmas Day?"

Mr Gates seemed disturbed, abstracted. But he still insisted.

"No, please. You might as well stay. I've enough for two."

"Two?" Hank asked. "Don't you mean three?"

"No," said Mr Gates. "I don't."

Hank followed the man into the kitchen. Mr Gates took a pitifully small, over-cooked turkey from the oven.

"The police came last night," Billy's father said, as he put the turkey onto the table.

"Last night?" Hank asked, confused. It couldn't have been about him then. "What for?"

"They came to tell me about Billy. Someone found his body, by a bin, in a Service station not far from London. Looked like he'd died of pneumonia, that's what they reckoned."

Mr Gates dolloped mashed potato onto two plates, followed by soggy carrots. Hank took the information in slowly. For the first time, he thought about the boy's pale skin, his empty eyes, and how cold the cab seemed when he was in it.

"So, what I saw was . . ."

"Aye," said Mr Gates. "It was. Mind you, I'm glad the little sod didn't come to haunt me. I never could stand him. He wasn't my son, you know. Oh, she said he was, but I never believed her. Brown hair and blue eyes weren't in her family or mine. I was well rid of him."

"He wanted to forgive you," Hank started to tell him.

But Mr Gates didn't seem to hear. He got out the carving knife and began to sharpen it, all the time ranting on about how much he'd hated his son.

"It was a good thing he left when he did, or I'd have killed him myself."

Hank remembered how Billy had tried to explain his father's actions, to account for what had made him the way he was. But Billy had been wrong, Hank knew that. Some people were bad. They were born that way. You couldn't change them, only make sure that they got what they deserved.

"Hungry?" Mr Gates asked, reaching for the whisky bottle.

"Very," Hank lied.

He reached over for the carving knife as Gates was getting the drinks. Billy's father raised his eyebrows as Hank pointed the knife in his direction, then shrugged his narrow shoulders and smiled as though nothing was wrong. For some reason, he seemed to trust Hank.

"You hold that knife like a man who knows how to use it," Mr Gates said, awkwardly.

"I've had a lot of practice," Hank admitted, with a wide grin. He moved a little closer to Mr Gates, who sloshed whisky into Hank's glass.

"Thank you," Hank said, in a cold, polite voice.

He stood up, as though to get a better grasp of the feeble bird beneath him. Then he turned to Billy's father, who looked suddenly uneasy. Hank moved a little closer, lifted the knife, and smiled again.

"Shall I carve?" he asked.

BURNING MEMORIES

Adèle Geras

he second thing my dad did when he heard that he'd got the job at Cedar House was buy me this notebook I'm writing in now as a celebration present. I've never had anything fancier than a red exercise book before, but this is a proper journalist's notebook, only with pretty flowers on the cover, the kind that makes you want to write down everything that's happening so that you won't ever forget it, and also all your secret thoughts.

The first thing Dad did when we came out of Cedar House after the interview was leap into the air (clicking the heels of his boots together) and shout "Yee-hah!" My dad shouts "Yee-hah!" whenever he feels at all pleased with anything, but it's usually a quiet sort of shout. This wasn't. This was a really raucous and triumphant "Yee-haah!!!" at the top of his voice, which startled some ladies who were on their way to the posh shops in Didsbury. I don't expect they get many honest-to-goodness Country and Western fans in this part of Manchester. I said so to my dad, trying to calm him down a bit, to make him behave himself.

"Guess you're right, Lou honey," he admitted, adjusting his black stetson and pulling his fringed suede jacket tight round himself to keep out the cold. "Ain't seen many Lonesome Cowboys in Didsbury village, no sirree."

Dad is not a Lonesome Cowboy. He isn't even American. I suppose he could be Lonesome, but the nearest he's ever been to a cow is a Tesco milk carton. He's just a person with a vivid imagination, and likes pretending he's in Nashville, Tennessee, strolling down to the Grand Old Opry, hobnobbing with George Jones, and Merle Haggard and all the good ol' boys, and buying drinks for Tammy and Dolly and Nanci in saloon bars filled with fiddle music and people in checked shirts. He loves Country and Western music. We play it all the time on our ghetto-squeaker ("too small for a blaster," says Dad), and I know all the songs by heart. He and my mother called me after Emmylou Harris ("the greatest of them all," says Dad), but when I got to secondary school, I told them my name was Louise. My mother had been gone eight years by then, so I didn't see her coming up to the school and putting them straight.

Dad and I don't know where she is. She's never been back, never written to me, never sent a birthday card or a Christmas card.

"She lit out and disappeared," my dad says wistfully, "just like a woman in one of those Country songs." My mother leaving made my dad worse. He spent more and more of his time imagining and dreaming and pretending and listening to his tapes. Somewhere along the line, as he puts it, he became properly divorced. The jobs he got became more and more grotty, and so did the flats and bedsits we lived in. I used to hate the holidays. At least at school there were people to play with and hot dinners.

Now we live in this enormous dilapidated house with about eight other people. It's called a Communal House, which means we share the rent and take turns with the washing up and the cooking. There's a big lounge for everyone, and a TV which sometimes works and sometimes doesn't. There's a wonky video. I don't care. I read books all the time. I joined the library with Dad when we came to live here. I couldn't believe it at first. They let you have all these books to read, and you don't have to pay for them. I love it.

I was slightly dreading Christmas, though, until Dad got the new job. We spent it here last year and it was awful. All the other people in our house had gone to their families, but my grandma and grandpa are dead, and Dad was an only child. The worst thing of all about last Christmas was that Affleck's Palace, where my dad had a kind of half-job, was closed for four whole days over the holiday.

Affleck's is my favourite place in the world. I suppose if you look at it one way, it's nothing but a market on three floors of an old building that used to be a department store called Affleck and Brown. On each floor there are small booths and little stalls and bigger shop spaces, all pushed in together, as if someone not very tidy was in charge of a crowded doll's house. But you won't find pies and sheets of greenish tripe and pigs' trotters in Affleck's. What you will find is second-hand clothes, silver jewellery, joss sticks, Doc Marten boots in every colour you can think of, velvet waistcoats, patchwork trousers, hand-painted T-shirts, amber beads the size of gobstoppers, crafts from Latin America and Africa, postcards, old records, Heavy Metal tapes, lace and chiffon scarves, hats made of velvet and a café where you can go and sit and sniff all the smells that are hanging around.

It's always crowded at Affleck's. Students roam around in packs and it's a good place to go when it's raining if you're homeless and hungry. It often is raining in Manchester, and I recognise the faces of some of the people I've seen begging at Piccadilly or in the Arndale Centre. Most people don't look at beggars, but I do. The young ones have grey faces and the old ones frighten me, because I can sometimes imagine my dad getting like them, singing his songs to the accompaniment of our ghetto-squeaker outside the Royal Exchange, with passers-by throwing change into a hat. His job at Affleck's isn't secure. Dad knows someone who makes these T-shirts, and he's helping him keep an eye on the stall for a few hours every day. That's all, and even though I can wander around for hours quite happily, the pay is dismal.

And then, this new job at Cedar House came up. Bill, the T-shirt man, told Dad about it.

"They're opening that Cedar House in Didsbury over Christmas," he said. "It's been done up nicely, and it's going to be a school sometime in the New Year, so they say, but just over Christmas they're using it for the old folks."

"Where do these old people come from?" I asked my dad, on our way to the interview. "It's not tramps, is it?"

"Oh, no," said Dad. "It's just that some old folks' homes close at Christmas, because so many people go and visit their families, and the staff need a bit of a break as well. This lot that are coming to Cedar House, well, they've got no one at all and nowhere to go."

I was going to the interview as well, because my dad had

decided that Mrs Brightson should see how clean and well-behaved I was, and what a help I would be around the place.

"Otherwise," he'd said, "she'll think the worst. If I say I've got a teenage daughter, she's going to imagine black leather and nose-rings, you betcha!"

As it happens, I'm small and my hair is long and fair, and I was wearing black jeans and my best jersey, hand-knitted Fair Isle that I'd found in Humana for £3.

Mrs Brightson liked my dad. I could tell. He was being less cowboyish than usual and I think she was impressed that a single father should have coped so well with bringing up a daughter all on his own.

"She's a credit to you, Mr Edwards," she said. "And I expect she'll be willing to lend a hand over Christmas."

I nodded demurely, and my dad got the job and said "Yee-hah!" and bought me this beautiful notebook. I've filled fifteen pages already. Tonight we're packing and tomorrow we'll be moving into Cedar House, going to that part of town where there are gardens and trees, and you never see homeless people with grey skin huddled in doorways, holding up bits of cardboard, asking for money.

Once upon a time long ago, Cedar House was a home for just one family. I can't think how they filled all the rooms. There were twenty bedrooms, arranged along corridors and up little staircases and around a kind of gallery. You can stand outside your bedroom and look down into the front hall below you. Even if there were fifteen children in the family, there would still be all the downstairs rooms to do things in. Cedar House had a ballroom, a drawing room, a library, a music room, a dining room and a billiard room. Mrs Brightson still called them by their long-ago names, though as far as I could see they were just plain old lounges filled with beige armchairs and sofas and a dining-room where the tables had orange plastic chairs all round them. The house was big and square and echoey on the inside, and the dozen old people who were staying over Christmas wandered through all the spaces, gathering near the gas fire in the drawing-room or round the colour TV in what used to be the library as if they were frightened of being anywhere on their own.

I was a little nervous of them at first. They seemed so wispy and small and wrinkled, and they walked so carefully every-where, as if they were afraid of breaking into small pieces at the least bump. Lots of them had fingers that looked like tree-roots. It was hard to imagine them striding about or running or cooking, or doing anything athletic. That's what I thought at first, but then they started to talk to me. I learned that Mrs Thomas was County Tennis Champion in her day, and Miss Ballantyne was a dancer once, and Mr Simpson

("You should really call me Sergeant Simpson") was a dashing soldier in the war and spent his time driving around the desert in a tank.

"I never realised," I told him, "that you all had such interesting lives."

"What we've got," he answered, nodding at me and poking the air with a gnarled finger, "is Histories. We've got a Past, every last one of us, but not much of a Future, eh? Eh?" He thought this was a really good joke every time he said it, but I only found it funny once.

Mrs Brightson was the main person in charge of the Senior Citizens, as she called them. Dad had to do all the handyman things around the house, and also be a kind of porter to check people coming and going. There were two helpers (ladies) who weren't exactly nurses or cleaning ladies, but something in between.

Then there was Ruby, the cook. As soon as I saw her, I thought: maybe this is the one. I ought to explain. Ever since I was four or five, I've been on the look-out for a mother. I haven't told anyone. I especially haven't told my dad, because he's tried so hard to be a father and a mother to me that it would be rude, I think, to say that yes, I've been lying all these years, and yes, I do miss my mother. I'm not as bad now as I used to be. I've got accustomed to it over the years, and a lot of the time I don't think about it at all, but at

Christmas it gets bad. All the ads on TV feature exhausted mothers in aprons spooning gravy over gigantic turkeys, or smiling dewy-eyed at their poppets opening The Perfect Present. I can't bear it.

I can't remember too much about my real mother. My dad kept some photos for my sake, but he's burned a lot as well. She smelled lovely, I remember that, and she seems to have been pretty and cheerful-looking. Not at all like a mother who runs away and leaves her husband and daughter. I used to think she went because of something I'd done, but my dad says no, it was just another man, like it is in the songs on our ghetto-squeaker. But why did she never get in touch? I wanted to know.

"Too painful for her, I expect," Dad would say. "The thought of you must be making her feel guilty."

She hated being unhappy, he used to tell me, and I'd nod as though I understood, and all the time part of me was saying: "But what about me? I don't like being unhappy either. It's not fair."

I gave up on my own mother long ago, but that doesn't stop me being on the look-out for a new, improved one. My dad has had some girlfriends, but not one of them has lasted long. He never says why, but I bet it's me. I think it's because they don't want me for a daughter, but I've never told my dad. He'd deny it. According to him, I'm the cat's pyjamas, and he doesn't see that other people don't feel quite the same.

Ruby, though, was perfect. She was good-looking in a comfortable, motherly way, with laughing blue eyes and a nice, cuddly sort of figure, and she never minded chatting, or letting me help her prepare the food. She seemed to be about the same age as my dad, as far as I could tell. Her work kept her in the kitchen a lot of the time, so she didn't come across my dad all that often, but I'd worked out that that might be an advantage. She could meet me first and get to like me ever such a lot, so that when she got to know Dad properly, she'd fall into his arms with a sigh and we'd all live happily ever after.

I tried hard to find out whether Ruby had a husband or not, without much success. For someone as talkative as she was, there wasn't much about herself she gave away. I kept opening my mouth to ask whether she had any children, and then closing it again – I don't know why.

"What're you getting for Christmas, then?" she said to me one day, and I said:

"I haven't bought it yet, so I don't know."

Ruby was chopping vegetables, but she stopped in mid-chop, and looked at me. I went on, hurriedly:

"My dad says he never knows what I want, and it's pointless wasting money on something I'll not be that

254

chuffed with. So I choose it. And I choose something from me to him at the same time. Socks, it is, usually. Sometimes I can find something a bit different."

Ruby shook her head, without comment, and I changed the subject, making a note to ask Dad for some money tonight. Christmas will soon be here.

I bought my present earlier today, and it's the most beautiful thing I've ever had. I can't wait till Christmas morning, when I unwrap it. I can't get over how lucky I was to have found it. At one point, I thought I wouldn't have anything.

I set out for town first thing this morning feeling like a millionaire. I had three five-pound notes in my purse.

"That's ten pounds on you, and five on me, and don't try and cheat or I'll know," my dad had said.

I hate Christmas shopping. There are too many people pushing and shoving along the pavements, too many tinny carols being churned out at top volume in every shop, and too much decoration, and glittery red and green, and stupid-looking Father Christmases with cottonwool beards half coming off. The least tinsely place I could think of was Affleck's Palace, so I went there. I knew a lot of the stall holders, and in 'Silver Bells and Cockle Shells' there were rings for ten pounds and under that I liked the look of.

As I got off the bus at Piccadilly, a thin, sleety rain began to fall out of the sky like a grey blanket. I turned up the collar on my coat and wished I had a scarf or a hat. I thought: why does it never snow here? It's not fair. The white flakes should float down and cover up the litter on the black pavements and then we would all tread on it as if it were a soft white carpet. Instead of which, what we get is needlepricks of icy sleet and a wind that could slice strips off a person's face.

I walked past Lewis's and crossed the road over to Debenham's, and then I saw them: a thin young girl and a dog. The girl was wearing jeans and a skimpy denim jacket. She had cropped hair and fingerless gloves and a face like a ghost. The dog was black and so skinny you could see his ribs. This girl wasn't even bothering to hold a sign up. She had squashed herself and her dog into a kind of alcove just past the optician's shop. My heart started thumping. I had all that money . . . it wasn't right for me to have all that money and for her to have nothing. The dog looked at me as I passed and made a whimpering noise in his throat. I took one of the fivers out of my purse and went up to her.

"Merry Christmas," I said. She didn't look much older than me. She smiled, then frowned.

"Are you sure?" she whispered. "It's a lot of money."

"Yes, I'm sure," I answered. "I've got enough. Truly."

Then she said a funny thing. I remember it because it's not the sort of thing you expect someone to say to you at eleven o'clock in the morning in the middle of a crowded city street. It was more what you'd expect to hear in church. She looked at me with very clear grey eyes and laid a pale hand like a claw on my sleeve.

"I know," she said, "that you will reap your reward."

After I'd left the girl and her dog behind, I felt good for a few minutes. I was a kind and generous person. I had made someone a bit happier, and that made me happier until I realised that now I only had ten pounds for me and my dad. I sighed. Bang goes my ring, I thought, unless I can find something really cheap for Dad. I felt bad the moment this thought came into my head, and I walked around Affleck's feeling guilty for a bit, not even looking properly at anything, just glancing about. Dad's present, it seems to me now, looking back, practically jumped up and waved itself under my nose shouting, "Buy me! Buy me for your father! I'm just what he wants."

I was looking at a tray of rings in "Silver Bells" and beginning to feel downhearted because there was nothing I liked and could also afford. Out of the corner of my eye, I caught sight of something. I could see turquoise and flashing silver, and I turned round to look properly.

"New stock," said Marymary, the owner of the stall. "Western-style ties."

I knew at once that Dad would love a leather thong that fastened at the neck with a turquoise and silver clasp. I looked at the price tag: £6.99. I bought one without a second thought. There were now three pound coins and one penny left for me, and it was all my doing. If I had a grotty Christmas present this year, I had no one to blame but myself.

"You look," said a voice from behind me, "as if you'd lost a shilling and found sixpence, as we used to say in the days of the Old Money."

I turned to see who had spoken to me, and there behind me was a stall I had never seen before. The name "Burning Memories" was painted on a sign hanging on the front of the counter, and the stall was about the size of three phone booths squashed together. The walls were hung with purple velvet and on every flat surface there were candles. I said:

"I've never seen so many candles before! Have you only just opened?"

The lady behind the counter considered this. In the end she smiled and said only:

"Here today, gone tomorrow."

She was peculiar, even by the standards of Affleck's Palace. I couldn't decide how old she was. Her hair was grey, but she wore it curling over her shoulders, like a young girl. Her arms were covered with bracelets from the wrist to

the elbow: gold snakes biting their own tails, copper bangles, and amber ones and some made of painted wood. Her clothes seemed to have neither a beginning nor an end. She was covered in layers of fabric that slid over her, and clung and floated and draped themselves around her body. She had bad teeth and hardly any wrinkles, and her eyes were clear and yellow, like a black cat's eyes. I shivered a little. This person was weird.

"What's your name?" she asked gently, as if she sensed that I felt a little frightened.

"Emmylou Edwards," I said, and added "I love your candles. I didn't realise you could have so many different kinds and colours."

"Delighted to meet you, Emmylou. My name is Clio, and yes, there are as many different candles as there are . . ." she looked around, searching for the right words ". . . dreams and desires in the heart, or memories in the mind. For every hope in your breast, I have a candle that will burn to make it come true. There are candles to make you forget, candles that can light a spark of love where no love is . . . oh, they have powers you could never imagine! There are shapes and colours to suit every occasion. I make them all by hand. Come in and have a proper look around." She moved aside and I slid in behind the counter. I thought: it's like a proper cave, and I was surprised that there was enough space for me and Clio to walk about in.

"It's bigger than it looks," I said.

"Most things are not what they seem," said Clio. "As you will discover."

"And there's so much . . . so much to look at."

As well as the candles, there were small bottles containing oils that looked like jewels melted down. There were crystals in a basket, blazing where the light touched them, and another basket full of marble eggs that were heavy and smooth to the touch. Perhaps, I thought, I should buy one of those. They were only £1.99. I had almost decided on a pink one, when I saw the candle and knew that it was mine with a certainty that seems stupid looking back. What if it had been too expensive? If I say the candle was green, that won't begin to describe what it looked like. It was a swirling mass made of every green in the world (seas, forests, leaves, grass, emeralds, jade, lime) moulded into a shape that was almost but not quite round. The surface of the candle had been carved into patterns that looked like plants or leaves or curling waves or small dragons. It was hard to work out what they were, but they twisted and crept all over the candle like living, growing things.

"I like that one," I said, pointing up to it, "but I expect it's too expensive. I haven't got much money left."

"This one," said Clio, "is very special. It's one of my scented range. Have a sniff."

She set the candle down in front of me. I bent my head to fill my nostrils with its fragrance, and it smelled of my mother. I had to have it. I said:

"It smells exactly like my mother, and I haven't seen her since I was very small."

Clio smiled. "It smells of the past," she said. "Wait till you light it."

"I'll never light it," I said. "I never want it to burn away."

"You must light it on Christmas Day," said Clio. "If you do not promise to light it then, I will not sell it to you. I shall raise the price so that you can't afford it, unless you promise me."

I sighed. Perhaps I should have the pink egg after all. At least I would still own it in January. Did I want a candle that would just disappear? Wasn't that a real waste of money? I don't know what happened to my common sense. Instead of saying, no, I don't want it after all, I said: "O.K. I promise. How much is it?"

"It's three pounds and a penny," said Clio. "By coincidence."

I stared at her. How did she know what was in my purse? The yellow eyes shone at me like lanterns, and I shivered. X-ray eyes, I thought, as if I were in a science fiction movie.

I shook my head to clear it of stupid thoughts, and then I emptied my purse out on to the counter.

"Have you got your bus-fare home?" Clio asked.

"Oh, yes," I said. "That's separate. That's not Christmas money."

"Good," Clio said. "Now I shall wrap your candle for you." She found some sheets of purple tissue paper and folded my beautiful present into them. The silence grew between us, so I said, just to make conversation:

"I like the name of your shop. There's a song called 'Burning Memories'. Waylon Jennings sings it. Do you know his songs?"

Clio shook her head. "I've heard neither of him nor of his song. Is it a sad one?"

"It's about this man, burning letters and photographs and things, burning everything that reminds him of his wife. She's left him, you see."

"A very sad song then." She smiled. "There you are. I've managed to find a carrier bag, which doesn't often happen. Don't forget your promise."

On the way back to the bus stop, the thought of the candle in its tissue paper wrapping made me feel warm inside. The girl and her dog had gone from the alcove beside the opticians. Perhaps they were having a lovely meal some-where in a café full of warm light and good food. The candle

262

in its carrier bag swung from my hand as I walked. Maybe this was what the girl meant. Maybe the candle was my reward, I thought. Oh, I wish it was Christmas Day tomorrow. I wish the time would fly.

Christmas Day is over. It's Boxing Day, which I always think of as a flat, featureless sort of day: like a Sunday, but worse. My candle is nothing but a hard puddle of green wax on a saucer, but it was worth it. We had, we all had, a magical time, a time that's busy disappearing from my mind already. I have to write down what happened before I forget it. If anyone else reads this, they probably wouldn't believe me. They'd most likely say: it's quite understandable at Christmas. You had too much to drink . . . ate too much rich food . . . it's no wonder you were seeing things. I haven't spoken to anyone about what happened. Maybe they know and maybe they don't. Maybe it was only in my head, and maybe not. I'm only sure of one thing: my candle made it happen. Whatever sort of thing went on, Clio knew about it. I know the candle was responsible, because until I lit it, everything had been normal.

Dad and I opened our presents early in the morning. The tie made him shout "Yee-hah!" as I had known it would, and he put it on with his pyjamas. He was a bit perplexed by my candle, but said in the end: "Well, if that's what you wanted . . ." and wandered off to shave and dress and get ready for breakfast.

We all ate together in the dining-room every day, and when I reached my place, there was a small pile of presents waiting there for me. I was so embarrassed, I didn't know where to look.

"Open your presents, dear," said Miss Ballantyne, and I blushed scarlet and started tearing paper off my parcels. Everything was quite small: soap and chocolates, and lacy hankies, but I felt as though I'd been given the most wonderful things in the world. Ruby had given me a £5 book token.

"Because you're always reading," she explained, and I was so pleased, I went over to where she was helping one of the old gentlemen to cut up his bacon, and gave her a big hug.

"Thank you," I said to them all. "I feel awful. I haven't got anyone a present, and I'm really sorry." There were cries of how it didn't matter, and that Christmas was for the kiddies, really, wasn't it? Then I said:

"But I'll share one of my presents with you at dinner time. It'll make everything really special." I didn't realise when I said that quite how special it would turn out to be.

After breakfast, I went to help Ruby with all the

last-minute things in the kitchen. She had a glass of sherry next to her on the working surface, otherwise I don't think she would have said anything. What she did say was:

"My daughter would be just a little bit older than you are . . ." Then she laughed. "I think of her most at this time of year. It's true, isn't it, what they were all saying? Christmas *is* for the kiddies. Most of the time I'm fine." Tears were pouring down her cheeks now. "Give us a tissue, Lou dear, and let's say no more about it. I expect it's the drink talking."

"Is she dead?" I asked. "Your daughter?"

"She might just as well be. I haven't seen her since she was a week old."

I must have looked puzzled, because Ruby went on:

"I gave her up for adoption. Everyone (the doctor, my parents, even me, quite often) thought it was for the best. The father . . . he was long gone. A lot of people told me it was the right thing to do, and I believed them. Give her a better chance in life, they said." She took another sip from the glass of sherry. "They were wrong, though, weren't they? I miss her, even after all these years. It wasn't so bad while Mike, my husband, was alive. I used to hope we might have children of our own, but now he's gone . . . well, it's too late, of course."

"You could marry again," I suggested, thinking of my father. "You could become somebody's stepmother."

A thought struck me, quite suddenly. As soon as Affleck's

opened after Christmas, I'd go back to Clio's shop and buy some kind of love potion. I knew, I just knew she would have one that would work a miracle. I cut into another Brussel sprout, and smiled to myself.

Christmas dinner was a very jolly meal. We all ate too much, and then I lit the candle, which I'd put ready on a saucer beside my plate. As the flame grew brighter, a thread of pale green smoke rose from the wick and curled up into the afternoon air. Up and up it went and you could see it clearly. It wasn't dispersing. It was making shapes up near the ceiling, like a ribbon of mist. I felt Time stretching out all around me. No one at the table said a word.

"If I don't close my eyes," said one of the old ladies, a Mrs Rosebery, "I shall fall asleep right here at the table."

"I know exactly how you feel," said Ruby.

"I could do with a spot of shuteye myself," said my dad.

Before I knew where I was, I was sitting all alone in the dining-room with the debris of our Christmas dinner in front of me on the table. Outside the window, it was already dark. My candle was the only light, and that was odd. Had someone switched off the electric light on the way to their afternoon nap? I pushed my chair aside, and picked up the saucer with my candle on it. I turned away from the table towards the window, and saw that the whole room was different. What had happened to the cheerful striped cotton curtains that were there a moment ago? Now, velvet drapes hung at the window, and I could just make out in the yellow candlelight, a crystal chandelier above my head. And the table with all the remains of our Christmas dinner – where was that? There was something very strange going on. I remember thinking: I'll find the others, then everything will be normal. I left the dining-room carrying the candle, and went upstairs.

I don't know how to describe what I found there. I went from bedroom to bedroom, knocking on the door of each one. No one ever told me to come in, but I opened each bedroom door as I went past and found (I don't know how to put it better than this) a scene from the past. I could tell it was that because everyone looked so young. I know they were real scenes that I saw, real memories brought to life, because when I went into my dad's room, there he was with me on his knee. I looked about two years old, and I was waving my new doll about by the leg. My pretty mother was smiling at me and blowing me kisses. I've still got that doll, only she's much older now. We were in our old house. I would have said I didn't remember it at all, but I recognised the patterns in the carpet, and there on the chest of drawers was the album cover of one of our oldest albums: 'Elite Hotel' by Emmylou Harris, my namesake. There was even a Christmas tree in the corner, hung with coloured balls and stars and small foil-wrapped chocolates. My dad looked happier than I'd ever seen him. I stared and stared at this scene, taking note of every single detail, so that I'd remember it to write down later, and here I am writing it down and already it's a bit hazy, like something I may have dreamed. But I didn't dream it.

As I shut my father's door, I heard someone singing carols in Mr Simpson's room. Perhaps, I thought, he's turned on the radio. The door was slightly ajar, so I peeped round it. Walls, ceiling, window: everything had vanished, and I found myself outside a rather grand front door, decorated with a holly wreath. Snow was falling. The flakes were actually settling on my shoulders. There was Mr Simpson. I recognised him, even though he was much younger. He was holding a lantern, and leading the singing. His voice and the other voices rose clear and true into the night sky. Suddenly, the door opened and the light made a golden triangle on the dark pavement. The carol singers went into the house, and I imagined mulled wine and Christmas cake, all marzipanned and iced and garlanded with red ribbons. I turned and found the door back into the corridors of Cedar House, and I remember wondering vaguely: where has Mr Simpson's bedroom gone? as I walked towards Miss Ballantyne's room. Would that be changed as well?

The old lady's door was closed, so I knocked, even though

I knew I wouldn't be answered. After only a second's hesitation, I opened the door. I was in a drawing room. There was a Christmas tree brilliant with candles in one corner, and people were sitting on sofas and chairs, obviously waiting for some sort of show to start. A space had been cleared for the performance. I watched a small boy reciting "Little Jack Horner" and a slightly bigger boy playing the violin. Then a younger Miss Ballantyne (she looked about fifteen) appeared in a white tutu and pointe shoes of pink satin. The shoes were so new that they must have been a present that morning. A lady in a purple dress sat down at the piano and played while Miss Ballantyne danced and twirled and dipped, and her white dress floated out all round her, and her shoes twinkled over the wooden floor. When she had finished, everyone clapped and cheered, and the little boy handed chocolates and nuts to all the guests.

I walked with my green candle from room to room, and in every one, someone was happy – happier than they'd ever been. Mrs Thomas was serving Christmas dinner to her children, those very same children, probably, who had arranged for her to stay at Cedar House this year.

I went to Ruby's room last of all, and there she was: a very young Ruby in her mother's kitchen, helping her sisters make mince-pies at two o'clock in the morning. They were

269

singing and giggling as they worked. They were happy. Everyone I had seen had been happy.

I went to my room and watched the candle, what was left of it, burn down to a pool of green wax. As I lay down on my bed, I thought: it's like seeing everybody's dearest memories, like holiday snapshots come to life . . . everyone's happiest Christmas, the loveliest pieces of the past, brought back for a while. I closed my eyes and slept.

I wasn't going to mention my candle, but a few days later my dad said:

"I don't know what Ruby put into the Christmas pudding, but I had the best dream ever that afternoon. I can't really bring it to mind now, but I know it was wonderful. You were tiny, that I can remember. Wow! I loved that dream."

"That wasn't Ruby's pudding. It was my candle. The smoke from my candle put everyone to sleep."

"Maybe they all had wonderful dreams too, you never know," he said, and disappeared before I could tell him that they had.

There's good news and there's bad news. The good news is: Mrs Brightson is so impressed with Dad that she's asked him to be the caretaker for the school that's going to open here in April. I shall have to change schools, but I don't mind. I'm used to it. When I was little, we moved all the time. Now that my dad has got a proper job, he might settle down.

The bad news is Ruby left before I could get to Affleck's Palace. She would have done just fine for my mother, if I'd had a little help from Clio. I mentioned it to my dad, and he laughed.

"I liked her well enough, Lou honey, but she didn't make my heart beat faster, and that's a fact."

As Dad spoke, a pleasant thought occurred to me.

"Is Cedar House going to be a girls' school?" I asked.

"Yes," said Dad. "Girls only, aged five to eleven. A preparatory school, Mrs Brightson called it. Very exclusive and expensive."

A very exclusive and expensive school would have lots of teachers. Maybe one of them would fall in love with my dad. I don't expect exclusive and expensive teachers notice caretakers very often, so I shall definitely need some help from Clio. Tomorrow, I thought, I shall go and ask her advice.

I went to Affleck's this morning. It was pouring with rain as I got off the bus and I was drenched by the time I got there.

No one I asked had ever heard of Clio, and "Burning Memories" was nowhere to be found.

I felt sad all the way back to the bus stop, but then I caught sight of the girl, the one I'd given a fiver to. She and her skinny black dog disappeared into Back George Street, and at once I felt happier, though I wasn't sure why. Maybe, I thought, Dad'll manage to fall in love all by himself without any help from a magic potion, and if he doesn't, well, we can manage on our own. The sun broke through the clouds as I got on to the bus and flashed and sparkled on every single puddle between Piccadilly and Cedar House.